Adelaide

Book 2 in Felicity

To Annie,

For when you are old enough to discover a whole new world of stories

ISBN: 9798431495403

<u>Other books by Faith</u>

Children's:

The Witch's Kitten (Misty #1)

The Broomstick Trials (Misty #2)

YA:

Felicity (Felicity #1)

Adelaide (Felicity #2)

~ Contents ~

7	Chapter One
21	Chapter Two
31	Chapter Three
43	Chapter Four
61	Chapter Five
81	Chapter Six
101	Chapter Seven
125	Chapter Eight
141	Chapter Nine
157	Chapter Ten
181	Chapter Eleven
189	Chapter Twelve

~ Chapter One ~

Adelaide Thorpe, if you are not familiar with our protagonist, belongs to three younger sisters: Felicity, Kitty, and dear little Phyllis. Their strong relationship had been developed in the many years in which they had played and worked side by side before Adelaide had left her beautiful country home in order to create her own family with a successful businessman, Nicholas Ramsey, who lived in the neighbouring town. Their union had begun three summers before when she was entering her 18th year in life, and he his 25th, and had initially been received with reluctance and even fury from her Great Aunt Augusta.

Lady Augusta, as she was known to the majority of Bath, had acquired a large fortune following the death of her husband a few years prior, and was considered an opinionated, and consequently troublesome, figure between the members of the Thorpe family, excepting of course Adelaide's mother, Margaret, who was so enthralled by the wealth and status of the old woman that she found in her heart more acceptance for her forward, and often rude, ways of conversing. Some level of ability in tolerating a conversation with her Aunt had Adelaide succeeded in attaining, and she often found herself mediating between her and her sister Felicity, as the two found themselves more often than not conflicted on one matter or another. Through this, Adelaide had fulfilled her duty as the elder sister to protect and guide the younger girls, even though at times this proved difficult.

Returning to the hesitation shown by Lady Augusta, she had verbally demonstrated her opposition to his status and youthful age on multiple occasions, yet the couple seemed almost unaffected by her resistance. In each other, they had found a trusting and content marriage, and for the romantic nature of their hearts, this suited them quite perfectly. And so, with a frowning personality sat rigid in the front row of the church, Adelaide Thorpe became Adelaide Ramsey and promised to stand by Nicholas for as long as they both shall live. With the exception of Lady Augusta, the church was alive with merriment and celebration, as the two walked arm in arm down the aisle towards the colossal doors and into the carriage, and the day had been spent with little thought of the miser, much to her own dismay.

Within a year of that joyous day, Adelaide and Nicholas were blessed with their firstborn. Looking down at the babe in her arms, she was met with small, delicate features and a prevailing sense of innocence in Katarina's eyes. Her soft features imitated that of her mother's, as well as her quiet temperament, yet Nicholas was the preferred parent as he spoiled her due to an abundance of love he had not the pleasure of giving to anyone but his wife and daughter.

For two years the three lived quite happily in their sizeable home, along with their two servants, in a town quite close to Adelaide's family; this pleased the Thorpe household as it meant that the sisters would not be separated to a great extent.

Our story begins on a day quite close to Katarina's second birthday, with the Ramsey's and Lady Augusta sat politely within the confinement of the parlour. The Great Aunt was sipping her tea at an immense speed; Adelaide had learned of the woman's mannerisms and their meanings long ago, and so she knew that her haste demonstrated that her Aunt had something of importance to tell them, and was simply trying to be courteous when offered the beverage before she began. And began she did:

"Now, Adelaide, you know how much I adore little Katarina, but don't you feel as though there is something quite the miss?" Adelaide positioned her mouth as though to speak, but was cut off before she could utter a syllable. "Not only would it be beneficial in Katarina's upbringing, but to have a boy would secure your family line and provide opportunity for the both of you! As you know, I, myself, birthed six strong boys, one of whom being your father, who, though sweet at heart, has no practical mind about him. Perhaps you better have two boys minimum."

"Aunt Augusta," Adelaide began, in the most tender voice she could manage, for that was the best way to communicate an opposing opinion to her visitor. "At the moment, we do not feel it necessary to bring another child into the house."

"Why ever not? There are only benefits for such an action; I am proof enough of that! You are at such a prime age for childbirth; you shan't be twenty and one forever." She placed the teacup down harshly, twittering away to herself in shock. "First, you marry without my blessing to a man below what you could have achieved," she began, husband and wife suddenly finding themselves blushing. "And then you refuse to provide for your family! It's disgraceful, and I'm sure that your mother would agree with me; that woman has such sense in these matters. Although, of course, I am still discombobulated as to how she could allow such a union as yours to happen! I would never have allowed my own daughter, if I had had one, to partake in such a demotion of status as has occurred here."

"I understand your thoughts on our marriage, Aunt Augusta, but the fact of the matter is, we are already married, quite happily so, and therefore, I do not understand what you expect," Adelaide managed, feeling as though the difficulty in remaining polite to her Aunt's standards had become almost impossible.

"I expect little, for you have promised yourselves to each other but what I do propose is a way to fix, in a way, what you have started. You shall need a son in order to carry on Nicholas' business, for Katarina cannot do so, and she will be of no use for another fifteen years when we can begin to find potential suitors for her."

"She will only be seventeen at that point?" Nicholas questioned. Of course, he knew that it was expected for girls to marry young, but Adelaide had been eighteen which he personally deemed a more appropriate age for marriage.

"Rather late if you ask me," the old lady began. "Perhaps I should begin my search a year earlier." Adelaide could not help but wonder if Lady Augusta would still be alive after another fourteen years, but the family had accepted that she was quite talented at defying death, and so the young girl assumed that questioning the likelihood would in fact be futile. "I expected some reluctance from the both of you, I must admit, and so I propose this: should you fail in providing a male heir, I shall remove you from my will, which, I can promise you, involves a considerable sum." Nicholas and Adelaide had never been materialistic in the slightest, and preferred to live a simple, though comfortable, life, and so this did not have the grand impact in which the old lady hoped to achieve.

"We shall think on it," Adelaide promised.

"I suppose that is all I can ask of you; the two of you never seem to be traditional in any sense. That being said, this was much easier than it was for your mother to find a husband for Felicity; now that girl really is trouble! I do feel sorry for the man," and she continued her twittering, Adelaide and Nicholas both trying to follow along, though equally unsure as to whether they were supposed to be listening; Lady Augusta seemed quite in her own world.

Until she left to return to her stately home, she spent the remainder of her time complaining of people and situations, making Adelaide and her husband quite uncomfortable yet unable to do anything about the matter. After a further three quarters of an hour, she found that she had exhausted as much as possible for the time being and requested her carriage be prepared so that she may return home to the relief of the young couple.

The company of the old woman was replaced with that of their two year old daughter, Katarina, who paralleled Lady Augusta significantly in both energy and optimism, as she bounded into the room which contained her parents as soon as she heard the closing of the door. Her coping mechanism for tolerating the Great Aunt was to avoid her as much as possible, for little Katarina was sometimes frightened by her loud and authoritative voice.

"Come here, little one," Adelaide said, reaching out her loving arms to hold her child close to her, grateful for the innocent smile on her toddler's face which appeared even more refreshing after having been with their tiresome guest for so long.

"Food," Katarina said.

"She has her priorities all clear," Nicholas laughed, tickling her before taking her from her mother to hold her himself.

"Daddy!" she chimed.

"Shall we go and ask the servants to lay out dinner?" he asked Adelaide, putting his other arm around his wife. The three of them appeared picturesque together, each smiling face presenting a member of the ideal loving family unit.

Only a little while later, a meal had been prepared and the family was sat around their quaint little table. Grace was said before Katarina excitedly ate as much as she was allowed, and Adelaide and Nicholas made sure every morsel had been eaten, for they both knew what it was like to survive on little and so they had found an appreciation for all that they had.

The meal passed not in silence, but in conversation, as the family believed in communication and developing relationships, rather than a strict code of conduct as one would expect at the dinner table. It was used as an opportunity to speak of the happenings of their day, for Adelaide remained at home with Katarina, and Nicholas worked in the office all day and sometimes into the evenings. It also, for this particular reason, was a large portion of the time that Nicholas had with his daughter to whom he was very much attached, and at times he even regretted being so passive in her upbringing due to his occupation, yet he knew that his wife was a wonderful mother and their daughter would want for nothing.

"I shall have to leave earlier in the morning, I'm afraid," Nicholas said, being reminded from his train of thought to inform her. "We have some new clients which could prove revolutionary to the company, and so there is a rather large amount of preparation to complete."

"Compete," Katarina repeated, a smugness clouding her face.

"Well done, darling," Adelaide said, encouraging any lexical attempt from the toddler, no matter how flawed. Then, turning towards Nicholas: "Would you wake me before you leave so that I may see you?"

"Of course I shall, for I could not leave to start my day without first spending a moment with my beautiful wife," he reached out for her hand to kiss it softly, their eyes alight with their love for each other.

"Eww!" Katarina squealed, creating a reaction of laughter from her parents. "Kiss!" she said.

"Now, I think that Katarina is perhaps ready for sleepy time," Adelaide said, removing her fingers from

Nicholas' clasp to pick the child up. "I shall take her to bed myself tonight." Nicholas nodded in response, watching in awe as his family left the room. He couldn't help but think back to what Lady Augusta had mentioned; he thought not of the will and the threat, but of expanding their family. He already had so much love for his little Katarina, and so he imagined having more children to give that same love to. Adelaide had grown up with three sisters, and having been witness to their close connection to one another, he wanted nothing more than for his own dear little Katarina to experience a similar childhood. Having little family of his own, he also wished to create a full and exciting setting in their home to accommodate his family-orientated nature which had been for so long neglected, though not due to his own fault.

~ Chapter Two ~

The following week, the Ramsey's found themselves once again in a church due to a marriage, yet this time they were instead seated in the front row and acting as witness to the union of Felicity Thorpe, Adelaide's younger sister, and a Mr William Giles. Adelaide had offered her sister some advice, which although turned out somewhat helpful, she still feared that she had intervened where she should not. Having been asked whether or not the marriage was suitable, she replied in a cluttered sense that in some ways it was, and in others it was not. Since a woman is only married once, and Adelaide had been lucky in that her husband had been the one in whom she loved dearly, she had no personal experience in arranged marriages, and therefore was also of a bemused view. However, her sister had requested her assistance specifically and so an answer had to be given. In response, that is, a rather muddled response, she decided that it was Felicity's duty to marry, yet in the process she should not lose sight of herself and her own aspirations. Believing this to be a strong compromise, the matter was settled, and her sister had devoted herself to that very task.

Now, only a few weeks since this conversation had occurred, were they attending the marriage in which they had discussed. Her sister stood tall and confident in appearance, yet she noticed small little clues of discomfort and fear. She wished that at the very least that she could be stood beside her, holding her shaking hands, so that she would not have to bear the dread alone, but she wished more so that Mr Giles would be a suitable husband and companion, and treat her as Nicholas treated herself. There seemed little hope in this in the current moment, for he stood apart from her, rigid and controlled; he did not even look toward her until they were told to face each other.

The wedding was completed in a structured and cold manner; all things were kept simple, quiet, and mundane to the extent that it was a very underwhelming celebration, quite dissimilar to their own. They had followed the couple out of the church, the small crowd gathering by the doors as Mr Giles let out his hand to help Felicity into the carriage. Adelaide felt at that moment that her sister may be in the depths of despair, and that, as mere bystander with no wealth, power, nor masculine authority, she could do nothing but watch and hope.

Moments after, Adelaide herself was helped into their carriage by Nicholas, with Katarina being placed beside her. Having been without supple entertainment for the hours that had passed that day, the little child decided to act in quite a disappointing manner for an adolescent who was usually relatively well-behaved. She was soon quietened by her mother, who required a little silence to process what this all meant for her dear sister, and women in general.

"What is on your mind, darling?" Nicholas queried, noticing the face she often acquired when thinking deeply on something. Knowing that she could speak her mind on any subject and only receive respect and support, she began:

"I cannot help but wonder about Felicity."

"I'm sure that is only natural, you have cared for her her entire life, and now she is less your responsibility, and, consequently, less yours in a sense," he said, hoping he had understood her concern correctly. “In some respects, she now belongs to this man more so than to your family, and as you are all so close, this may seem quite intrusive. Yet, I hope you remember that after our marriage, there was no drastic change. Of course, you saw each other a little less than usual, but you often visit them, and them us; with Felicity it shall be the same.”

“But we have no knowledge of this man; with you, I knew you well, I loved you. Felicity has only been in his company once before and she did not speak too highly of him.”

“Perhaps she was exaggerating; she often does,” Nicholas suggested.

“That is true, I had my suspicions, I must admit,” Adelaide confessed. “Yet, I feel as though I shall be more comforted once I speak with Felicity next. Of course, there is a fear that should he not be of the decent sort; she shall be bound my matrimony for as long as she lives, and I will be of no use."

"Your mother is sensible, if not a little terrifying at times," he laughed. "My point is, she would not abandon your sister to any man; he would have to meet her standards."

"Mother's standards consist of wealth and status, not of the heart," Adelaide said.

"As does the majority of society's, but that does not mean that she would give her blessing to someone who did not deserve the companionship of her daughters."

"I believe you are now just trying to present yourself in a higher esteem, are you not?" Adelaide teased, receiving a smile in return. "I hope my sister will have as wonderful a husband as I do."

"Perhaps a 'nearly' is required to make the situation possible, for I can't imagine a better husband than I," he said, posing grandly, causing a little entertainment for Katarina who had been frowning in the corner. "Try to put your mind at rest, dear, at least until you hear from Felicity, for she will confide in you either way. In the meantime, we have Katarina here to play with and pass the time!"

"Felicity has no one," Adelaide said, looking quite aimlessly out of the window at the fields.

"She has her family, and she has the promise of new friendships; in that sense, she has quite the abundance of people," his words comforted her immensely, but were not adequate in relieving her of her sisterly concerns, for it is not easy to forget eighteen years of friendship.

"Perhaps I should invite Felicity round for tea next week," Adelaide though aloud.

“If that would help, then I think it to be a wonderful idea,” Nicholas said, hoping that her nerves would gradually fade over the coming days. However, Adelaide’s mind was preoccupied with the thought that only a few hours prior, she had been assisting her sister with wedding preparations, including helping her dress and securing her hair into a suitable, yet practical, fashion. Felicity had then been unwed and a free woman, yet now she was a wife.

“I do hope that Felicity shall continue with her aspirations, as any woman should do, for though it is not expected, it is necessary,” Adelaide said. Nicholas had believed the conversation to have finished already, and so he listened with slightly less patience than before.

“Think of other things, Adelaide,” he replied. “Your mind may wander freely back to your sister when there is information to ponder on, but for now, there is merely nothing other than assumption and paranoia."

"I suppose you are correct," Adelaide admitted, not meeting his eyes.

"I may be correct, that I will confess with an ego, yet be assured that I know how difficult it is for your mind to think of other things," he reassured her. "Once you are settled with our usual daily schedule, your mind will not have the time to sit concerned over things that cannot be helped." He meant for it to be of assistance, yet it was not received in such a way. Adelaide decided that although grateful, she was quite unable to set her mind aside for the moment, and she believed it to be part of her sisterly duty to keep it within her conscience.

"Home!" Katarina excitedly squealed, bounding up and pointing out of the window at the house.

“Keep seated until the carriage stops, Katarina, there’s a good girl,” Adelaide said, returning forcefully to her duties of mother. The small child obediently did as she was told, but remained in better spirits than she had been with the promise of home and all that it entailed. Adelaide decided that she would spend more time with her daughter that afternoon so as to keep herself occupied and Katarina was relatively pleased with the attention bestowed upon her.

~ Chapter Three ~

Having spent the night attempting to sleep, and with failure, Adelaide had emerged from the bed with a tired composure and little motivation to begin the day. Nicholas, however, had slept perfectly fine, having no sister to concern himself with, and so he woke up feeling refreshed as he so usually did. His wife watched in jealousy as he easily rose from the bed and began to dress with an energy almost equal to their daughter's. On finishing, he turned to his wife, who sat on the bed with her legs dangling down the side and her head resting in her hands. Stretching out his own hand, he pulled her to her feet and gently kissed her forehead. The two met each other's gaze, him looking down at his love, and her up towards his beautiful smile, both content. It was moments such as these that had the consequence of memories of their courtship all those years ago; they had both been so young but not naïve, as would have been expected, for their love really was true and their wanting to marry seemed the best option for everyone involved. Even Margaret Thorpe, overly concerned with prosperous marriages as she was, rejoiced at their asking for a blessing, and was all too helpful in the preparations for the wedding.

Adelaide thought specifically of the moment in which the two kindred spirits had first spoken of their feelings for the other. It had been an autumn day, almost four years prior, and they had spent time in each other's company many times in those past few months, for there was a large array of balls in succession in a short period of time. They had been sat in the parlour of Thorpe Hall, Adelaide cross-stitching and Nicholas speaking of business with her father, when Aloysius had been called to help assist Margaret in some matter of importance, leaving the two friends alone. For a minute, neither one dared break the silence, for they had never been as alone together as they had been then. Due to this sense of unknown, both began to speak at the time, which caused Adelaide to blush as she combed a strand of hair behind her ear and Nicholas to chuckle.

"You go first," Nicholas prompted; he was met with direct eye contact from the beauty who appeared so meek and silent.

"I was going to inquire after your business, Mr Ramsey," she said.

"Please, call me Nicholas," he began, rising to take a seat on the chaise next to her. Adelaide felt that she could not face him, for the only time she had been close to a man before was during dancing, which, in a room filled with people, was of no importance. “Business, though I expect you have no real interest in it, is going well. Perhaps you could tell me of what you are stitching?” his forward manner did not seem imposing to the young girl and so she was more than obliged to talk of her current occupation.

“It is for my sister, Felicity,” she pointed to the delicately stitched letters spelling out the name.

“That is very sweet of you, if I may say so,” Nicholas said, sliding closer with the excuse that he may see it better. Adelaide turned her head towards him, realising all at once how little distance there was between them, and their faces seemed almost touching. She watched his eyes slowly glance down at her lips before he composed himself, facing away and instead at his clasped hands in his lap. “There is something I feel I should tell you.” Adelaide gave no response other than placing her stitching work aside to provide him more attention, sensing that they would discuss a serious topic. “Over the past few weeks, I have found myself in anticipation of being in your company. An overwhelming sense of care and adoration is what I feel for you, and I would like nothing more than for you to be mine.” On uttering this last word, he lifted his head nervously to look into her eyes, hoping that her physical response would tell him what he longed to know.

“I must confess to being of a similar opinion,” Adelaide said, softly. She had never experienced anything of a similar nature, and so she was unsure of how to act, or indeed what to say, and so she decided that if she said less, she had less opportunity to say something wrong.

"Then, if I were to ask for your father's blessing, you would consent to being my wife?" he asked, the eagerness alive in his eyes.

"I would love nothing less," she said, smiling innocently.

She rarely thought back to this moment, for so many new memories had been created and along with them, more responsibilities that allowed less time for remembrance. However, when she did, she thought of it fondly and was temporarily transported to the mind of her eighteen year old self.

"I hope you and Katarina have a wonderful day, I shall miss you immensely while in the office," he said, holding her tightly, regretful that he could not stay in bed with her longer. "Goodbye, my love." He kissed her once more on her forehead, gazing intently into her eyes before quitting himself from the room, leaving his wife alone to begin her own day. For Nicholas, his days were usually different and unique, each one bringing new opportunities for the expansion of the business, yet for Adelaide, each day consisted of the same schedule, one which although she appreciated, she also at times wished for a momentary lapse in the structure so as to catch her breath. However, no break was in the realms of possible, and so she began to dress for the day with help from one of the maids, and her day resumed its usual form.

The day passed at a slow speed, for entertaining such a little child throughout the day while completing housework was quite a draining task. Adelaide motivated herself by remembering that her mother had managed the same thing, yet she had three more children, and so she felt that she could not complain. Instead, she tried to find the enjoyment in the activities. Katarina was spoiled with a picnic in the garden for their lunch, and was shocked when her mother began to chase her across the grass, for it was more playful than what the toddler was used to. Adelaide found it to be a good method of distraction from her sister's predicament, and, although exhausted after the hour spent in such a manner, she was quite content to continue her day with a more positive attitude. As a consequence, Adelaide and the servants prepared a light meal together to be served at dinner, as Katarina was minded by the maid, and the three laughed and enjoyed themselves immeasurably in the process.

"Nicholas will love this meal; it contains all his favourite foods," Adelaide said, though to one in particular, for really she only thought aloud. In some sense, doing things for the man she loved was a way in which to improve her own mood, as she would be witness to his smiling eyes when the food was laid out in front of him.

However, quite the contrary occurred on his arrival, as he entered through the front door in a quiet and sheltered array, only pretending to smile for the moment in which Katarina greeted her father for a cuddle. Adelaide ushered the child away with the maid, for she was lost in anticipation of learning what the causation behind his solemnity was. She looked to him with concern in her eyes, taking his hand in hers to offer support.

"I have bad news, my dear," he found that he was unable to look directly into her eyes as he told her, mainly due to the shame he felt, and partly because he believed he could not bear to see the pity her countenance would betray. "The new business opportunity did not go as planned; we lost vast amounts of finances that we invested."

Although Adelaide knew little of the business, she felt the fear of poverty alongside him, and questioned internally what this would now mean for their household. As though reading her mind, Nicholas continued: “We may have to make some small changes in the coming weeks until we can find some way around the problem,” he said.

“Of course,” Adelaide said, gripping his fingers tighter. “Whatever we must do, we shall do. Do not worry about me, Nicholas, for Katarina and I will be just fine,” she added, knowing her husband would feel guilty when he had no reason to.

“Thank you; I must admit I have no inclination as to what this will mean for the company as of yet,” he said, relieving his mind of chaotic thoughts.

“I am sure it will all work out,” Adelaide suggested, trying to provide advice as he had done for her the previous day. “The world often has a world of doing just that.”

~ Chapter Four ~

The following days consisted of plans being drawn up throughout the day by Adelaide as to what could be sold, while Nicholas worked long and hard hours at the office, each working towards a solution. Katarina struggled to entertain herself during this period, but, though Adelaide already had too much on her mind to concern her, she spared as much time as she felt suitable with her daughter. As a sister of four, spending time with those she loved was embedded into who she was, and she could not bear for Katarina to suffer any more than she must in the current predicament. It was for this reason that more time was spent between Nicholas and his daughter in the evenings when he returned from work, both husband and wife treating the child as though they were not facing financial struggle.

The first item to be sold for a considerable profit was a painting which had been acquired by Nicholas only the year before. Having been hung above the desk in their study since its purchase, the wall now appeared empty, and Adelaide feared that their home would continue to sink into an empty abyss and their sales would result in merely walls and basic necessity. Nicholas had worked for years in order to create a home for them, and now that home was being torn apart into small pieces that were being homed elsewhere. Having had the stability of a home which dared not change throughout her childhood, and then the easy transition from the first house to the next, she was not entirely experienced with changes to her surroundings to such an extent as this, yet she knew that she must keep a brave countenance whenever she was in the presence of Katarina, and even in her husband's company so as not to worry him.

Unavoidable upset was caused only a few days following the financial crisis' beginning, when Katarina watched in dismay as objects were passed through their front door. Now, dear reader, I must remind you that at two years old this house was all she knew, and strange men with strong arms were taking parts of her world with them, and the small child had no understanding of the reasoning behind it. Therefore, when the toddler's tears echoed down the bare hallway, her mother came straight away to cradle her and tell her that all was well. She spoke in her most tender voice to soothe Katarina, and after only a minute, her countenance was nothing but smiles.

Nicholas had returned sometime in the late evening, and having been preoccupied with noting finances in the study, Adelaide had not been aware of his arrival. Consequently, when the door to the room she was sat was opened, Adelaide found herself in shock at the noise, for she had been so focused on the sums.

"Ah, there you are!" Nicholas said, walking with a strong purpose towards his wife. Adelaide turned around at the sound of his voice, and, initially preparing to greet him, she was silenced by what was in his hands. "How has your day been?" he asked, standing behind her chair, leaning down to kiss her softly on the head.

"Quite fine," she replied. "May I ask why you have this?" she turned her eyes down to the object in his hands. Clasped between Nicholas' fingers was a small chest which had a gold clasp, the details both delicate and intricate. On her questioning, he placed it down on the desk in front of them both and opened it to reveal a handful of jewellery. To Adelaide, the chest and its contents was of a large importance, for it was a treasured family heirloom, and, though she rarely wore the necklaces, their significance was still of an immense nature.

"Now, this is just a suggestion, so please keep an open mind," were the words he chose to begin; words which Adelaide feared the purpose of. "The value of these would help us considerably, and we could stop emptying the house of our belongings."

"But these are *my* belongings," Adelaide argued. "To me, they are more valuable due to their sentimentality than anything else we could sell. I do not wish to part with them." As her eyes looked to them, her mind wandered to the moment in which they were first given to her. It had been soon after her wedding, or, more specifically, the first visit to her family home after the union had occurred. Her sisters had stolen her company throughout the first few days of her being there, but on the third day, she was asked into the parlour by her mother and father. After Kitty was told to find something other than listening to their private conversation in order to entertain herself, Adelaide was seated with her parents. Her mother, Margaret, appeared in an excitable state as usual, while her father, Aloysius, was seated in a sensible and unemotional position.

"Is there anything the matter?" Adelaide asked, sitting straight and polite. She watched as her mother could not keep still on the chaise as she looked toward her husband as though begging for permission with her eyes to be the one to speak first.

"I feel your mother will burst if I do not let her tell you," Aloysius said.

"Oh, thank you, dear!" Mrs Thorpe said, her rejoice demonstrated through the clasping of her hands. "Now, first of all I must express how pleased I am with Mr Ramsey; what a wonderful and successful man he is! It is only a shame that he did not visit with you, for we could have had such fun! I'm sure the girls would love to see a real life husband in their very own house!"

"Margaret," Aloysius said, urging her to hurry along with what needed to be discussed.

"Right, yes, yes, of course," the woman began again. "Just one more thing before I tell her," she ushered to her husband. "The both of you are welcome here at any point; in fact, we would love for you to come again in a few weeks. Oh, and bring dear Nicholas with you! We must make him feel quite at home here. Now, now, yes, I will begin; Aloysius, you need not look at me like that! Adelaide, dear, dear, Adelaide, your father and I have something for you," she finally concluded. Margaret elapsed quickly from her seat, unlocked the cupboard stood in the corner of the parlour, and brought out a small chest. "It belonged to your great grandfather, and your father and I have decided that now that you are married and quite the young lady, we would like to pass it down to you." She passed it to her daughter with a dominating sense of pride on her face. For Mrs Thorpe, securing her daughters in states of matrimony was of the utmost importance to her, and, with her first child, she had succeeded; her optimism for the other sisters was considerably less, but she took an internal note of her achievement with Adelaide. "Open it up, dear!" she prompted. Adelaide, with a much gentler movement than that of her mother, released the golden clasp, and found inside an assortment of necklaces. There were not many, but the value of the jewellery was all too obvious and she daren't touch them lest she cause some damage.

"They're beautiful," she said. "Thank you, both of you, I'll take good care of them," and so she had. For her, they'd demonstrated her fulfilment of duty as a daughter, and, as someone who prided herself on doing her best to please people, this was a wonderful triumph for her.

Being transported back to the current moment, Adelaide looked from the chest to her husband.

"I would much rather hold onto it, if it may be possible," Adelaide inquired, hoping that although she presented a compromise as it sounded as though she would part with them if necessary, he would still realise through her obedience that she wanted only thing. Nicholas could see this, for he loved her dearly, and could not bear to cause her any more discomfort than what she was already exposed to.

"It was a terrible idea," he laughed. "Do forgive me; I fear I am losing my wits the longer our problems continue."

"I cannot blame you, but I can remind you that though we are struggling financially, we are still in abundance concerning love," Adelaide replied, taking his hand in hers.

"That is true. Speaking of which, how has Katarina been?"

"Difficult at times, though I feel she is coping better than us," Adelaide admitted, regretting her words as they fell from her mouth.

"You are not coping well?" he asked, concern painting his face.

"I did not mean for you to know," she said.

"Adelaide, you are my wife; it is my duty to make you happy and keep you safe. If there is something damaging either of those, then I deserve to know, for I cannot help you if you do not tell me." He spoke only truths, Adelaide knew that, but she felt that she should not burden him further. "Please." She also knew that she did not have it in heart to disobey him, for his eyes seemed so desperate and worried.

"Do not think too much into what I say, for it is merely based on my not being used to change," she began. He nodded in response. "I have found the workload a little difficult at times, for between caring for Katarina and findings ways in which to save money, I have little time to breathe. Yet, I know it shan't last too much longer so I am quite content to continue as I am."

"I apologise for the stress that I am causing; I mean neither you nor Katarina any harm," he said, visible stress appearing through the medium of his furrowed brows. "I can make no promise of a particular day for all to be well, and with that being said, I thank you greatly for your willing cooperation; it is much appreciated."

"There is no thanks to be given," Adelaide said, cupping his hands in hers. "I am your wife. Katarina and I are your family and therefore we must remain optimistic and enthusiastic in our domestic endeavours." The conversation continued with a similar agenda, the specificities told to both with a sense of completion and astonishment in their realisation of how much had been done. However, the topic became instructed towards a long term solution after a few moments:

"Perhaps we should reconsider the offer, if we may call it that, given by Lady Augusta," Nicholas said, grieving as he spoke. "Though it shall not directly help us in our current affairs, it may help our children avoid what we have faced; surely it is our duty to provide them with any financial aid possible?"

"I suppose it would be of use to Katarina, for a marriage based solely on wealth could perhaps be of less importance if she has some small wealth of her own," Adelaide thought aloud.

"Of course, and as her parents we must always have Katarina's best interests at heart," he began. "The only concern I have at this current moment is that we cannot finance another child. It is already struggle enough with one."

"That is a valid worry, Nicholas," his wife said, unsure of how to console him. "I am sure, if we are careful with our expenditure for a while, one more child would not prove difficult to too great an extent. Compare it to what it would result in, and it seems as though we have no reason not to. Aunt Augusta will be all too happy and I imagine that she would provide some support although I must stress the importance of keeping our struggles explicitly between the three of us, that is, yourself, I and Katarina."

"Is it wise to assume a two year old is capable of understanding the importance of secrecy on such a pivotal matter?" Nicholas questioned."I suppose our denial in spreading word to your family will be of some use though; we do not want shame to be brought into our household."

"Oh, Nicholas," Adelaide began, disbelief flooding her thoughts. "My family would not put shame on our situation; I know all too well the abundance of assistance they would provide for us."

"Then why are we not to tell them?"

"It is unfair," she answered. "They still have two children to care for with Felicity and I married, but less suitors to marry them to. I do not envy their position and I could not wish to apply any strain to their household when we have solutions and ways in which we can aid ourselves. We must not learn to look elsewhere for help before looking in ourselves."

"I feel the poetics in your sister has influenced you some," he laughed.

"Felicity has influenced me in many ways," she admitted, taking a moment to think of her sister. "I do miss her."

"It won't be too long until you are reunited once again, for no one could separate the two of you even if they tried." Having not yet met Mr Giles properly, Adelaide still had a slight fear in relation to her sister's marriage, yet, their own struggles provided a barrier to these worries for the time, and she could not help feeling a little grateful in the midst of their disorder.

"So," Adelaide murmured, taking her mind away from her sister. "What are we do about the will?"

"If we are in agreement, we must comply," he suggested. "Adelaide, dear, I feel as though I must tell you something."

"Yes?"

"We are not having this child solely for a financial benefit and to please your Aunt," he began. "We are doing this in hopes of expanding our family. Please, try and remember that, for I would loathe to know that you felt nought but guilt if we do this."

"I understand. We would no doubt have had children anyway; this circumstance has merely changed the timeline."

"Precisely."

~ Chapter Five ~

The following day brought with it a guest; Lady Augusta had returned to follow up on her proposition, confident that Adelaide and Nicholas would only be too happy to comply after having had time to think upon the offer. She was met at the door by the maid servant, whom she had no recollection of a name, and was lead into the parlour and greeted by Adelaide alone. Having called in the early evening, Nicholas was not yet home and not due for another half hour. In being told this, the old woman insisted on waiting before they spoke of anything of importance, and the time was filled with gossip she had acquired over the previous few days and, when she had found her mind to be quite dried up of any more, she turned to small talk of the weather and other mundane matters.

The half an hour in which they waited passed relatively quickly for Lady Augusta yet painfully slow for Adelaide. Strong attempts were made to appear interested and polite, though her efforts were ignored as the old Lady spent no more than a mere second at a time glancing at her, distracted instead with her language.

"Lady Augusta!" Nicholas came through the door, still in the process of removing his gloves as he did so. "I heard you had arrived; I do apologise for keeping you waiting but I thank you all the same." Lady Augusta rose to greet him in the proper manner before seating herself again.

"It is no worry! Adelaide and I have entertained ourselves with some wonderful conversations, haven't we dear?" Adelaide nodded submissively in response. "Yet, now that you are here, we may move on to the some more significant matters of urgency. I presume you have discussed the will?"

"We have, Lady Augusta," Nicholas replied, knowing better than to continue talking.

"Then I suppose I can be expecting a new addition to your household relatively soon?"

"That would be correct."

"Ah! I knew my offer would be too beneficial to pass up! Of course, I do have such a way with words also that would make it too difficult to refuse!" Her pride seemed almost comical to the couple and in consequence, silence and a straight face were the priority in which to focus on as she continued in her smugness for a few sentences more.

"There was something else, Lady Augusta," Nicholas said, avoiding the questioning look from his wife beside him.

"Yes, dear?"

"We were wondering if it would be shameful to ask for some short term financial assistance?" A moment of hesitation appeared on the woman, before her hands were clasped and joy was plastered upon her countenance.

"It would be my honour!" Her excitement was extraordinary.

"That is such a relief to hear, Lady Augusta; we are so very grateful." Never before had the Great Aunt seen such genuine appreciation and her willingness to help only increased. However, upon viewing the somewhat sullen appearance of Adelaide, she became both confused and concerned; why did she not have the same indebted air about her as her husband?

"Adelaide, is there something amiss?" she questioned, her eyebrows furrowed, though quite without meaning to be.

"All is well, Aunt Augusta, thank you," was all she could manage.

"Well, in that case, smile dear child!" she said, offering the first show of happiness. Adelaide responded how she was expected.

"Now all is sorted, both short term and long, and I fear I must continue my errands; there are an abundance of neighbours who would value my visiting them on such a fine day."

Lady Augusta had left the residence surprisingly quickly in comparison to her usual exits, but had left the couple in some strange predicament. Fortunately, or perhaps not for his wife, Nicholas could find no difficulty in bringing the problem to light in conversation only a minute after their guest had left.

"Pray tell me the reasoning behind your brooding features? You almost embarrassed us and what is worse, you nearly caused your Aunt to combust!"

"I did not want my family to know; you knew that and you still did it," she said, simply.

"I know, but as the man of this household, it is my duty to provide for this family," he began. "I cannot do that right now to the best of my ability and it hurts me and it embarrasses me. You will never understand how it feels to have that sense of responsibility thrust upon you and how it is when you cannot live up to it."

"Yes, I do!" she cried, shocked at his selfish answer. "I am a mother, and a wife! Every day I must devote myself to the two of you; raising a child is not easy, nor is it something that can be put off until the next work day! For weeks, we have watched our home being torn apart, knowing that I cannot do anything except help Katarina and support you as well as I can."

"It is not the same."

"Of course not, but your duty does not diminish mine, and I fear you are too immature and arrogant to see as much."

"Immature? Arrogant? Speak to me as you usually do, I beg of you."

"I converse with you now in a sense of desperation and disappointment, whereas there is usually a mutual respect between us. I shall not play the role of perfect wife while you subdue my very being out of existence, as I would not for you." She tried to turn and leave the room, for she found difficult in speaking back to him despite how truthful it was, but he would not let her.

"Stay," he said, his voice quiet but strained. She hesitated but could not find it in herself to face him. "Please accept my apology." She gave no verbal response. "I am stressed, that is all."

"We all become stressed from time to time, but we should find it in our good morals and hearts to not shun those who provide us support."

"Beautifully said and I wholeheartedly agree," his voice grew ashamed. "Please, forgive me, and let's continue to the evening in better spirits." Without answering his request, she left the room.

No further conversation occurred between the two that evening, nor for the following few days. The most that had been said was an agreement to attend a ball planned for the week after by some relatives of Nicholas.

This ball came relatively slowly into existence, for the days became a lonely abyss the more they continued their silence with one another. Having lived with a social family consisting of four sisters, Adelaide had not grown used to such a quiet household, and Katarina looked at her parents with questioning glances in which her mother was too saddened to realise.

Katarina, being of too young an age to attend the ball, was to reluctantly stay at home. She found some redeeming enjoyment in watching her mother prepare as she gazed on the dress in admiration, not having seen her mother in such exquisite attire often. Adelaide herself felt somewhat uncomfortable seeing her appearance in the mirror and for a moment believed it better to remain at home, and, had not a sudden motivation to show the appearance that was all fine, she would have done just that.

Since the carriage ride was filled with only silence and an uncomfortable air, I shall not trouble you with the details of subtle glances and grimaces and instead shall continue our story from the arrival at the residence in which the ball was occurring.

Nicholas, despite not quite wanting to, held out his hand to assist Adelaide from the carriage, and a small smile of gratification was shared between them both, which was met with a giggle of childish and romantic delight from Nicholas' younger cousin who had excitedly ran from the dwelling to greet him. She was met with an informal embrace as his wife watched submissively from behind.

"Oh, how I have missed you so very much, Nicholas!" the young girl cried, clutching onto his arms.

"Not as much as I have missed you, little Clara," he replied. "Would you do me the honour of allowing me to escort you to the ball?"

"Oh, yes, I'd adore that! But, what of Adelaide; who shall escort her?" Nicholas turned to face her for only a moment before giving a response:

"She will follow." This answer quite suited the young child and so the three entered into the social event. Adelaide forgot all her woes with her husband the moment she entered the hall, for it was so beautifully and elegantly decorated that her mind could think of nothing more than the candles and delicate features. Despite her maturing age, she felt as though she was young once more and back home at Thorpe Hall with her sisters, basking in their youthful natures.

"Come dance with me, Nicholas!" Clara demanded innocently, pulling on his arm. He obeyed with little disinclination and left Adelaide to stand to the side of the main method of merriment by herself. With the motivation to appear a submissive wife, she bore this with little physical strife, and instead tried to interest herself with her surroundings which, with a similar level of imagination to her sister, Felicity, she found to be of easy attainment with little effort on her part. Time was spent in this manner for the duration of two dances, when, just as the third was beginning, Nicholas returned, though this time with the absence of Clara. He held his hand out, his fingers shaking a little with the nerves, and spoke to her with his eyes.

Adelaide, confused as to what she should do for a moment, hesitated before placing her dainty hand in his and allowed him to walk her to the centre of the room where the other couples had already begun to dance. In joining this other couples, Adelaide fell into the familiar rhythm of the dance, and found a relief in the movement, despite having to meet her husband's face of guilt throughout. For both, this moment reminded them of the first ball they had attended following their union, where they had danced so much that all other persons in the room had almost been forgotten completely. It is as times such as these, when a sense of nostalgia roots itself in a creature's very bones, that feelings of forgiveness tend to rise to the surface and, since Nicholas had much to feel guilty for, and Adelaide much to forgive, their dance created one of these moments. Though no words were spoken aloud, much was conversed between them in the midst of violins and cellos and, come the end of the piece, they bowed and curtsied not solely to mark an ending, but also to indicate a beginning or a progress.

The remainder of the evening was spent relatively apart, for Nicholas took advantage of surrounding himself with his family and Adelaide used the opportunity to befriend some young women who had attended who she had not previously had the pleasure of being known to. Having been confined to the household with only their few servants, a husband and a child to communicate with, she appreciated the change in scenery and situation to a great extent. She found herself able to discuss topics she had usually not the pleasure too, for there were certain subjects which she could by no means mention to Nicholas due to a lack of understanding, yet, within this plethora of femininity, she could structure the agenda of their conversing to ideas of motherhood, small entertainments and matters more trivial than that of politics and finances she assumed her husband would be talking of. Within a quarter of an hour, she had been enlightened on the husbands and children of all four of her new acquaintances and had spoke a little of her own.

"Are you the sister, then, of Felicity Thorpe?" asked one, upon learning of Adelaide's former home. She responded with a curt nod. "Then you know of Mr Giles? I hear he is quite wealthy. Do you know whether he has any siblings?"

"I do not believe he does, though I am merely the status of stranger with him," she answered honestly.

"Terrible shame," and that was the last on the subject. To Adelaide, it seemed odd for the conversation to change in so short a time, but she found herself more so entertained in speaking of other things to think of referring back.

Nicholas had noticed his wife centred in the small multitude of women and, after questioning for a moment why so many girls did not care to dance, carried himself to the crowd.

"Good evening," he said to them all, bowing his head politely. "May you be so kind as to relieve Adelaide to myself?" The wives curtsied in their compliance, and watched in awe as Adelaide took his hand to lead her away.

"They are such a beautiful couple," one remarked, as nods and demonstrations of agreement were given.

Nicholas had led Adelaide from the room completely to a secluded seating area in a hallway where the hum of percussion could only be faintly heard. Feeling as though he did not want her speak first, she followed in obedience and sat next to him.

"You were right, Adelaide," he began, the disappointment in himself clearly imprinted upon his countenance. His words made Adelaide feel as though she was the one in the wrong, although of course she was not, as she loathed to see him in such a low mood. She placed her hand on his in an attempt to show him that all was well, but he continued his apology, feeling as though he owed her more explanation. "What I did warranted no other response from you, that is, you were completely reasonable in how you reacted. I should not have done it how I did, but despite this, in hindsight, I still feel as though the assistance from Lady Augusta will be highly valuable to us both."

"I know, and I agree, though unwillingly and under a disguise of pride," she replied.

"We all are liable to give in to pride from time to time," he said. "I, myself, am guilty of it, and so it would be rather hypocritical if I were to hold it against you. Besides, my going against your wishes is the severe circumstance of this all."

"You thought you were doing the right thing."

"I did, and I do, but you are part of this family too and I should have listened and given you my full support," he decided. "Oh, Adelaide, will you forgive me?"

"Of course I will, for it would be silly to hold a grudge over you as a consequence of such a trivial matter," Adelaide smiled. "I hope we can use this to our advantage and learn the importance of communicating with each other and following through on what is discussed."

"That blow is certainly deserved so I shall take it with honour," he said, understanding the passivity in her hope. "Perhaps we should return home, I fear I cannot dance any longer."

The carriage home was much more pleasant that its predecessor as the glances were now innocent smiles much like the ones first shared in the early days of their union and the thoughts were majorly happy and content.

On arriving, the house was quiet and would have consequently been assumed empty had the presence of their sleeping daughter and servants not been known. Their entrance, therefore, felt wonderfully youthful as they crept through the halls all the while holding hostage laughs and giggles at inconsequential matters and comments.

~ Chapter Six ~

The following week, although spent in bliss and happiness, was unfortunately interrupted by a letter addressed to Adelaide that brought some rather terrible news. Fearing it could possibly be in relation to Felicity and Mr Giles' marriage and domestic life, she eagerly opened the envelope with no hesitation and found something much worse than expected.

Dearest Adelaide,

In strong reluctance, I regret to inform you of the medical condition of your sister, Phyllis. Only yesterday she contracted some unknown disease and has been bed-

ridden ever since, with the Doctor being in little hope of a recovery. I have contacted Felicity also and would like to extend an invitation to you to return home for a while in support of your sister, for these coming weeks may be the last she is blessed. I hope to see you soon and I apologise for being the one to share with you such melancholic and unwanted news.

Your Father.

In a clumsy state, Adelaide seated herself, the letter held between shivering fingers filled with dread. Nicholas had been in the room with her, though at a distance, and had watched in anticipation with a surprising abundance of patience as the letter was read. He now sat beside her, and, unwilling to ask to read the letter himself, applied himself entirely to his wife and in assisting her. Placing the letter aside on the corner table, he pulled her close to his chest, allowing her to cry into his chest; not knowing what would be most appropriate to say, he said nothing at all.

"It is Phyllis," Adelaide gulped after a minute. She began composing herself, removing her body from his enclosure as she continued to explain. "She has fallen gravely ill. Father has asked I come home for a time."

"I'm so sorry to hear that," he said. "When will you leave?"

"As soon as it is possible," her eyes fastened themselves tightly on the leg of the table as she begun to chain herself in her own thoughts. "Tonight would be far too soon to be adequately ready to any decent extent, but what if, by leaving first thing in the morning, I have unknowingly spent her last moments?"

"Fear not, Adelaide, for all shall be fine."

"I must fear, for there is no situation which be more appropriate for that very emotion! She is my sister, my blood, my heart! You cannot understand our connection, nor do I blame you for it, but I am valid in my concern!" She looked to the letter again almost in an aimless passion, and, upon noticing the date in which it was written, rose into further panic. "The letter was written three days ago! Phyllis could already be on her deathbed and here I am, not by her side; I must leave straight away." She carried herself from the seat, Nicholas catching her arm in an expedient response.

"You cannot leave now, Adelaide," he said.

"Why not? Every moment I spend here is another moment not spent with Phyllis."

"It is not safe to travel overnight, and Katarina is sleeping; surely you would not leave her here, for I shall be at work each day, and you cannot wake her now?" he said.

"I did not think," she confessed, feeling quite lightheaded at the realisation.

"No, you cannot think when you are in this state," he said, loathing how controlling he sounded. "Let me carry your load a little; you don't have to bear this alone." She nodded, though still felt worried to a large extent. Nicholas also was of a concerned state, but felt as though he must disguise this to assist Adelaide as well as he could. He sat her back down, and then called for some tea to be served in hope of some benefit to her interrupted breathing. The tea, though it came with an honest attempt of improvement, had little effect, and the night was equally disappointing as it brought with it no sleep for either.

Morning came far too slowly but when a reasonable time was reached, Adelaide began to ready herself for the journey with no hesitation, even waking little Katarina who rose befuddled and confused.

"Morning?" she asked.

"We're to have a rather early morning today, little one," Adelaide said, beginning to dress the child. "We are to visit your Grandparents." Undecided as to how to explain to such a youthful and innocent creature the current predicament, her conclusion for the moment was to say little at all and hope that all would be revealed as intended.

"Play with Kitty and Philly!" Katarina giggled excitedly, consequently making it extremely difficult for her nightgown to be pulled over her curls in a delicate manner. At this, Adelaide took a moment to assess internally as to how best to reply in order to cause the least stress, so much so that she considered whether or not Katarina should join her at all. Futile was this deliberation however, as with Nicholas working so busily and only the servants to care for her, there was no possibility in her remaining behind.

"Phyllis is a little tired, but I'm sure that Kitty would only be too happy to play with you," she replied.

"Philly plays better," said the little girl, confident in her declaration.

"I'm sure she does but she cannot play this week," *or ever again*, Adelaide thought to herself.

"Cry?"

"No, no, I'm fine." With Katarina now dressed, her mother wiped her eyes quickly and began on the other tasks that were required to be completed before they could leave.

The carriage ride to Thorpe Hall consisted of a similar degree of difficulty and Adelaide wondered if her daughter had always been so inquisitive and talkative, or if she was only just noticing it now as a result of shying away from sociality. Almost everything was commented on, from the new, scratchy curtains that had replaced the old ones to a new sign on the post office, and Mrs Ramsey had to rely on every muscle of patience her body held in order to successfully pass the journey with avoiding tears from the toddler; there would be plenty of those in the coming days and so if any could be avoided in the current moment they should be.

As the vehicle arrived at the land surrounding Thorpe Hall, Katarina excitedly rose from her seat, pointing excitedly at the abundance of trees and thatched roofing which she only ever saw here, for their residence was further in town, with a tiled roof and less greenery. Adelaide looked on her with envy, wishing she could find excitement in returning home as she usually did, but this visit was incited by a promise of death and the necessity to appear almost unaffected so as to keep spirits as high as it was deemed possible for such a circumstance.

The carriage door was opened by Mr Aloysius Thorpe as it reached the house and Adelaide gratefully took his hand. Katarina was lifted from the vehicle afterwards and greeted personally by Kitty who embraced her rather tightly that the small child giggled; she always forgot while at home quite how much attention she received when here and so was more than content when she was led by the hand to play with Kitty. On the contrary, Adelaide was not quite as content and fearfully began the conversation which must be spoken of:

"How is she?"

"Not well, I am sorry to say it," he answered, leading her down the path which led to the back of the house. Hidden between trees and looking over a small stream was a petite wooden bench in which they usually sat on her visits and this was no exception. "The Doctor has little hope of any improvement." A moment of silence commenced, both unsure of how to continue after such a fearful statement. "I'm not sure how many days we will have with her." Adelaide turned to him and found herself tearful at seeing his physical reaction; his eyes were struggling to remain strong and his jaw was clenched in a tight manner. In a small attempt to console him, she placed a hand on his, gifting a smile.

"Then we must make the most of what we do have with her and show her just how well she is loved."

Father and daughter sat quietly for a time, somehow finding the pastoral nature of their surroundings to be peaceful enough to claim some level of authority over their emotional states. Although only temporary, it was much appreciated by both parties but was forgotten once entering the house; the atmosphere there was not as forgiving as the beautiful outdoors.

"Oh, dear, sweet Adelaide!" Mrs Thorpe embraced her daughter eagerly before she had even left the doorway completely and then shuffled through to the parlour without stopping to breathe: "I am so pleased you decided to come! I knew you must have arrived when little Kitty brought Katarina in and, though I could not find you with her, I realised you must have been with Aloysius when I could not find him either! Oh, you must see Felicity, for she is around here somewhere, though she gets up to such mischief still! I uselessly believed that once she settled into married life, she would become more sensible and quiet in her ways, but she is just the same as she always was! Though, I suppose it is better for her to be healthy with too much sensibility than ill with none. Poor Phyllis; heaven knows why she deserves such a fate as this!" And thus the old woman resolved into a fit of tears. "What shall I do without her? What shall we *all* do without her?" A shadow of horror crept over her face at this thought, though she had thought of little else in the previous few days and so really her surprise was unnecessary. "She really is the most perfect child. Out of all four of you, she showed the most promise – her skills required of a housewife were exquisite despite lack of practice."

"Don't be blind to her limited looks," Adelaide had not noticed Lady Augusta perched in the corner, pursing her lips over Mrs Thorpe's best china, and struggled to acquire enough strength to hide a slight grimace, for she knew all too well that her presence would only make the coming days more difficult. "Even Felicity has a prettier face than her; that being said, pair the two together and you'd have the perfect daughter for marriage."

"Oh!" Mrs Thorpe cried, nestling abruptly against Adelaide's chest. "My little Phyllis will never be a wife!" Adelaide knew that there were, of course, more pressing matters than matrimony but once her mother fell into a stream of emotion such as this, there was no talking her into a sense of stability and logic. "Why must she leave us so soon? She was such a wonderful and promising girl!"

"Was?" Adelaide laughed. "She is still with us and with that comes hope! Don't despair quite so soon," she lied, partly for her own benefit as for her mother's. "Shall we go seen her? I have missed her terribly and have waited in anticipation to give her my love."

"Yes, yes, of course! I should have taken you to her as soon as you arrived!" Adelaide followed her mother as she hurried up the stairs, then, in almost the opposite manner, stopped abruptly outside the bedroom door, and in a hushed voice said: "try to talk quietly; loud noises could be disastrous for her." Adelaide nodded in understanding as Mrs Thorpe opened the door to reveal Phyllis piled under an array of blankets with a ghostly shadow over her countenance.

"Phyllis?" Adelaide whispered, walking slowly towards the bed. Her sister opened her eyes in a delayed flutter, her pupils surrounded by a red soreness that made her seem already halfway to Heaven. A failed attempt was made to reply to her sister but no words successfully came;

instead, a mere moan elapsed from her lips that concerned the other two beings in the room. In nervous uncertainty, Adelaide exchanged a look with her mother, who nodded cautiously to illustrate all was fine. Seating herself in a chair placed purposefully beside the bed, Adelaide held onto her sister's hand which was purple with cold; never had she been so physically close to death and she was so terrified of facing it that it took all her strength to not let go of the icicles in which she held. "I'm here."

Mrs Thorpe watched from the doorway for a moment, more quiet than I have ever known her to be, before leaving them to be alone. Composing herself on the other side of the door, she took a deep breath, wiped the hint of a tear that had begun to form, and continued on with some chores so as to distract her mind.

A melancholy hung over the household for the following few days, not one soul quite knowing how to brighten a conversation or moment of silence, and Phyllis had to endure watching her family mourn before she had even left this world, without, unfortunately, being able to tell them how much harder it made it for her. As family-oriented as she was, seeing her parents and siblings in such low spirits when she especially was the cause hurt her deeply, and she wished with all her remaining strength that she could tell them to all be happy. Alas, she could not, and so Phyllis was unfortunately relatively unhappy in her final days.

On one particular day, when Lady Augusta had left quite unexpectedly due to some urgent business with her estate, the family decided to take advantage of the time in which the Great Aunt could not control their activities to have a little merriment. Since a piano could not be brought to the bedroom, nor could Phyllis be brought to a piano, it was determined instead that the family would sing to her, for the sisters had often sung together throughout their childhoods. Phyllis, though it was a little loud for complete comforts with certain melodies, endured the pain and enjoyed it immensely, wishing that Aunt Augusta would remain busy with her estate much longer, for the smiles she saw were much more to her liking than the morbid frowns she had grown used to.

Though she could not verbally give her thanks, she managed a small smile which erupted much bigger smiles and embraces from those around her.

"Oh, Phyllis, you are so very brave," Adelaide said, combing her hair back from her fore-head. "Is there anything else we can do?" No answer came but Adelaide could not be sure that it was on purpose. “Would you like some water?”

“How are we to know what she means?” Kitty asked innocently.

“How about some form of code?” Felicity suggested. “Two blinks for yes and one for no?”

“That’s a wonderful idea, Felicity,” Adelaide said, turning her attention back to the sickly figure below her. “Would you like some water, dear Phyllis? Remember, two blinks for yes, one for no.” Two blinks, though weakly done, were given, and a glass of water was placed at her lips. Adelaide felt she was finally being of some use to her sister and decided to stay by her side as much as possible to assist her and keep her as comfortable and entertained as possible.

Unfortunately, as brave and selfless as this decision had been, Phyllis had passed away the following day, though not alone, for her family had all been around her. In fact, Phyllis met it bravely, finding a relief as she let go, though her family took it less so. As her eyes closed, Mrs Thorpe let out the deafening weeping she had been holding back so that her daughter would see only smiles as she departed, and fell into her husband's arms. The girls comforted each other, embracing and kissing.

~ Chapter Seven ~

Reluctant to remain at Thorpe Hall any longer than necessary while all she craved was her husband's love, Adelaide left with Katarina two days after the funeral, and was grateful for the quietness of the carriage. However, it was as though every inhabitant of the town was aware of their loss, for she lost count of the many fingers which pointed at the carriage as they returned home. Towards the end of the journey, the curtains had been closed, so that Katarina was the only person in which to pay attention to; she had much less energy than those on the other side of the walls, and, though not quite understanding what she had recently witnessed in relation to Phyllis, she mimicked the sadness that she felt in those around her.

A while later, the carriage came to a stop and the door was held open for the mother and daughter to leave. Nicholas was stood ready to greet them and Adelaide gratefully allowed herself into his arms.

"How are you?" he asked.

"Tired," she admitted, honestly.

"Let's get you both inside; you can tell me in your own time of what happened, though I fear I already know," he led them gently into the parlour, where refreshments and biscuits were laid out for their arrival. "I struggled to focus on anything while you were gone and so I avoided work today and instead prepared myself some little trifles which would ease your return." He looked proudly at the array of biscuits, almost as though he had done more than take them from the kitchen and laid them out on a tray. Katarina was extremely excited by the prospect of food and helped herself to a handful as her mother exchanged an appreciative glance with her father.

"Thank you, Nicholas," she said.

"Would you like Katarina to be bathed?" a servant asked meekly from the doorway.

"That would be wonderful, thank you," and so Katarina was led away, leaving husband and wife alone. Silence thrived between them, neither one knowing how to approach the looming topic; it was Adelaide who ventured there first. "Phyllis passed away; it was a lovely funeral."

"Oh, Adelaide, darling," he tightened his grip on her hand. "I wish I could have been there to support you."

"I had my family; I was not alone," she said.

"Despite that, I also had support I could have given to you and I must apologise for not attending to that," he admitted. “Is there anything I may do for you now to ease your mind?”

“You have done enough twice over, Nicholas,” she replied.

“Not in my eyes, dear Adelaide,” he began. “No; in mine, I did less than what you deserve, for you deserve every ounce of my effort and on this occasion, I gave you this to no degree. I propose to you an oath; to stand by your side, as I intended to do from the start, and care for you.”

“Oh, dear Nicholas, you do that in every moment of your being, can’t you see? You are always there for Katarina and I. We have been struck with grief, and so the stress, though likely to cause some problems, will not be permanent. In fact, I already feel all the better for being home with you; just seeing your face has calmed me immensely.”

Nicholas stepped as close to his wife as he could, cradling her small fingers in his which were wore and aching from the work he had been exposed to in the previous few weeks. Seeing hers, almost equally as poor quality as his own reminded him of how much he could not provide for her.

"I must admit that, although I am grateful for your feeling such a wonderful way, I will also commit to more. I cannot spend all my time at the office while my family are home. I vow to change my priorities, Adelaide." Her face was home to confusion.

"Our priorities right now are to become financially stable once again; time for family can resume after all is well," she said, reassuring him as well as she could do. His eyes fell loosely to the floor, his countenance displaying only disappointment in himself. "Better times will soon come."

Happiness was to be found quite easily the following day. Though Nicholas had left for the office as early as was required, Adelaide and Katarina had an eventful day, for the morning consisted of preparations for dinner, and the afternoon promised an activity of baking, in which the toddler had pleaded upon their doing after the biscuits the day before. The ingredients had been purchased before lunch and they were now laid out upon the table. Adelaide had baked cookies an array of times before and so she relied comfortably on the recipe within her mind, her thoughts guiding them through it. Katarina, too young to be much help practically, found enough enjoyment in stirring the ingredients in the mixing bowl.

“Someone at the door, Mrs Ramsey,” the two were interrupted by the maid.

"I'll be two moments, Katarina," Adelaide said as she followed the maid towards the front door. Left alone, the child was not quite sure what to do at first. After a moment's hesitation, she stepped down from the stool and went to explore. Upon doing this, she found some papers that had been left by the side door.

"Ingredients," Katarina decided, picking them up and taking them back to the table with her. She clambered back onto the stool and threw the papers into the mixing bowl, grabbing the wooden spoon and stirring them around. "That doesn't look right," she said, tilting her small head as she looked at her creation. She looked at the other ingredients around the bowl, trying to remember what they had put into it. The flour looked familiar, and when she glanced into the bowl, she could see a clump of it sat on top of the paper. Deciding they probably hadn't put enough flour in; she lifted up the sack and began to tip it. However, small children are not well-known for their motor skills and so, as you would quite imagine, the entire sack of flour now found itself in the bowl, the entire pages of paper buried deep underneath the white blanket.

"Katarina?" Adelaide came back into the kitchen, and did not notice the mess in the mixing bowl until she was stood directly in front of it. Caught in a state of confusion, she was consequently unable to move or speak.

"It looks wrong," Katarina said, prompting her mother for help.

"You've used a whole sack of flour!" Adelaide said, trying her utmost hardest not to raise her voice. "And what's this?" she questioned, noticing the corner of a page peeking out of the mound.

"Paper."

"Paper? Where did you find paper?" she asked. Her daughter pointed towards the counter next to the side door, not quite understanding what was happening. Adelaide pulled at the corner of the page, sliding it out from under the flour and dusting all the remnants away. She could just make out a few numbers and part of a graph. "This is your father's paperwork!" Panic rose through her as she tried to save the other pages, laying them out in a row on the table. Her attempts felt futile, however, and she sank into the chair, unsure of how she was going to tell Nicholas. What if they were important?

"Cookies?" Katarina asked.

"We can't make the cookies, anymore," Adelaide said, calmly, knowing that her daughter would not have ruined the papers maliciously or even purposefully. Katarina began to pout her small lips, her eyes shining and blinking up at her mother. "I want cookies," she said, sadly.

"It was my fault, I should not have left you alone," she admitted. "We will make cookies another day." The small child was saddened upon hearing this, but her attention was placed elsewhere rather suddenly when a squirrel climbed in through the window. Unsure of how to remove it from the room herself, Adelaide called the maids to assist her. Katarina found the entire ordeal amusing and was subsequently entertained for the following half an hour.

Fearing the quality of the paper that had found itself in the mixing bowl, Adelaide spent the afternoon trying to return it to its original condition but the attempt was futile. The ingredients marked almost every piece of the pages and they were crumpled so much so that the documents were rather difficult to read. She hated to admit defeat but there was nothing more to be done. In disappointment, she laid the pieces out in a row on the desk in the office to avoid further destruction and decided to tell Nicholas of the ordeal when he returned home that evening.

Of course, the residence of guilt within her stomach made the rest of the afternoon pass by painfully slowly. It seemed an eternity or two before Nicholas came through the front door, hanging his scarf and coat by the entrance with a smile upon his face as though everything was perfectly fine, but, of course, for Adelaide, a smile could not even be imagined upon her countenance. Her face was sullen and anxious and Nicholas noticed as soon as their eyes met before he had even left the hallway.

"Adelaide, dear, what is the matter?" he walked up to her with an air of concern, his fingers gripping softly onto her arm. She looked at his hand in an attempt to avoid his eyes; she did not dare to see his worry when she would most likely cause him distress as soon as the story was told. "You can tell me." His reassuring words were not futile but they did not make the task of admittance any easier than it had been.

"Katarina and I were making cookies earlier in the afternoon," she began.

"Oh, is that all?" Nicholas laughed. "You had me worried! That seems absolutely wonderful! I hope you haven't eaten them all!"

"No, that's not all," she said, biting her lip in anticipation; he seemed so happy and content to be home from work and here she was with some terrible news! Nicholas returned to the same worried countenance as before. "I left for only a moment; it really was not long at all!"

"Is Katarina alright?" he asked.

“Yes, yes, she’s fine,” Adelaide began again. “When I returned, she had found some papers of yours; they must have been left here this morning by accident. I think she mistook them for ingredients, for she had mixed them into the bowl. I tried my hardest to clean them but the mixture is rather sticky. They are laid out in the kitchen,” she felt somehow worse despite telling Nicholas the complete truth. “I’ll show you what I managed to do.” Nicholas followed her to the kitchen and glanced at the papers. She really had done a wonderful job, for, although they had only a few hours before been piled under cookie mixture and scrunched to large extents, they now sat somewhat flat. Picking one up, Nicholas glanced at the contents of the page.

“I hope you didn’t tire yourself out too much trying to undo Katarina’s mistake?” he asked, still reading through the page. “These are unimportant, I promise you. They were merely rough copies.”

“I still feel utterly awful; I am so sorry, Nicholas,” she said. Nicholas placed the page back down with the others and created a pile.

“Don’t be,” he kissed her on the forehead and smiled down at her. “You worry enough for the both of us at times and it is not necessary.”

“I know,” Adelaide smiled, shaking her head at herself. “I suppose it comes from being the eldest sister; there was always so much pressure.”

“I hope you don’t feel pressured now? I am here for a reason, you are aware?” he said. “I love you, Adelaide. I chose to marry you and in doing so, I chose to protect and care for you. I can carry our burdens for a while. Why don’t you visit Felicity tomorrow? You have not seen her for a while, and perhaps having one of your sisters close by for a few hours will help in relieving some stress."

"I think I might and Katarina can stay with the maids. I'll be back in time for dinner, though, for Katarina is sometimes quite difficult when asked to eat." They both laughed, each remembering moments when Katarina's stubbornness became clear. "Will you be home for dinner, tomorrow?"

"Perhaps, though I will not know for certain until I see how much work is to be done."

"Ah," she said, trying to hide her disappointment.

"As soon as all is well financially, we shall all take a holiday and spend countless hours together," he said, embracing her.

As planned, Adelaide departed from their home in the late morning in the carriage and began her journey to the neighbouring town. She had not been away from the house in such a while that each tree and blade of grass seemed much more exciting than it had done before and she found herself in anticipation of seeing her sister once again. Of course, she was also nervous of the possibility than Felicity could not be home at all, for she did not know of her visit. This worry subsided as she left the carriage and saw her sister walking round from the side of the house.

"Oh, Adelaide!" she called, her excitement as youthful and extreme as it had always been. She held onto her bonnet as she skipped to her sister who stood by the carriage.

"Dear, Felicity," Adelaide said, finding herself in a tight embrace.

"Oh, I have missed you ever so much! Do, come inside! I'll send for some tea and biscuits and we can talk!" The two sisters hurried into the house and then the parlour where tea and biscuits were brought only a few moments afterwards.

"How are you," Adelaide asked.

"I suppose I am alright, how are you? I have not heard from you in so long; I was beginning to believe that you had forgotten all about me!"

"It would be impossible to forget about you," she replied. "Nicholas and I have a few household issues but we are handling everything as well as we ought. I must admit I have been a little overwhelmed recently, so Nicholas suggested I visit you."

"Oh, so you needed to be probed by your husband to be even inclined to visit your dear little sister?" Felicity laughed. “Sometimes I feel as though I myself am too overwhelming.” Her demeanour became much more serious rather quickly but Adelaide was accommodated to her sister’s feelings and often extreme emotions. “Part of learning to be a wife is also learning how to be calm and composed, although I have so much energy within me. It is quite difficult.”

“Being a wife is a little difficult at times, that much is true, but it is also very rewarding. I find myself lucky to have Nicholas, for really I feared that mother would marry me to any man who earned a certain fortune a year the moment he offered. Although I do not know much of William, I believe he can’t be too awful.” Thinking upon their two situations of marriage, Adelaide wondered at how miraculous it was really that she and Nicholas had even married at all. She remembered the opposition that Lady

Augusta had first enthralled upon them and how her mother had hid her own disappointment under the excitement born from her first child marrying.

"I suppose it is easier now than it was at first," Felicity contemplated. "It's so strange when I pause for a moment to think upon how things have changed in recent years. Firstly, you left to marry Nicholas, and although I adore him, it really did begin a series of events that could no longer be delayed. Once you had gone, the pressure of marriage was passed unfortunately down to me."

"Don't look so sad, Felicity," Adelaide said. "You have a beautiful house with the most wonderful garden. Why don't we take a walk outside before I leave?"

"You have not finished your tea?" Felicity questioned. Adelaide had always been so proper as to finish her tea, especially during a visit.

"I remember how much you loathed the fact I would not leave until I had finished the cup," Adelaide smiled as thoughts of the two of them when they had lived at Thorpe Hall came to mind. "I suppose things really have changed."

The garden was as Adelaide had described it to be; it was simply wonderful. Since late spring was in the air, the flowers were in full bloom. Shades of blue, purple and reds were scattered across the horizon, for the greenery seemed to expand in a never-ending state. In comparison to the Ramsey's garden, "The Mansion", as it was named by its previous owners, was a palace.

"How is Katarina?"

"Stressful," was the response.

"You make having children seem so – oh, so," Felicity pondered. "I think I have become quite speechless." Adelaide looked towards her sister in astonishment.

"You, speechless?" she asked. "It is impossible! Firstly, you always have something to say, no matter the topic or how inappropriate a time it is. Secondly, you are a writer; words are your sorcery."

"With William so engaged, I have little opportunity to talk to people," she began. "Perhaps I am out of practice?"

"Perhaps that is the oddest thing I have heard all the week," Adelaide replied. "I must admit, I am very glad I came today. Sometimes a girl really just needs some time with her sister."

"Oh, Adelaide, that is the sweetest thing!" was the response. "I often wish Phyllis was still here; there is so much to tell her." The air between them did not become stiff as expected, but rather, it became filled with the realisation that both girls had needed to talk about their sister. "She had so much left to do with her life."

"Then we must live ours with her in mind," she decided. "It is only normal to miss what once was, but we shall her again. In the meantime, there should be little time dedicated to mourning, and instead, we should remember her as though she is still among us."

"Are you quite certain?"

"I am not," Adelaide replied. "Yet, I feel it may be the easiest and happiest solution."

"That is true, though it is an unwanted solution all the same."

"Unwanted or not, that is what we have." The two girls felt much better following their short conversation on Phyllis but neither expected another to appear for quite some time. Though both have agreed to think as though their sister was still alive and well at Thorpe Hall, neither found this easy to do so quickly and so the conversations were turned to something of a more positive nature for the remainder of the visit. They spoke of Katarina and Nicholas and Felicity's changing life with William and such wonderfully happy things that when it came time for Adelaide to return home, for she really had left it as long as possible, the two were not quite ready. The carriage had been called for to be prepared and so the few minutes that this took were spent with embraces and kisses between the sisters.

"Do come again soon, Adelaide," Felicity said as she helped her sister onto the carriage.

"As soon as time allows it, I shall not hesitate," was the reply.

~ Chapter Eight ~

Weeks passed almost swiftly due to the busy state that all in the Ramsey household found themselves in. Nicholas had been working long hours at the office, even on Sunday afternoons. The extra time put in had made a significant difference, for the figures were slowly rising. However, Nicholas felt that if he decreased his efforts for even a moment, they would return to their prior situation and all would be lost; he was, as a consequence, motivated by a fear of failure. His wife, knowing him more closely than even his family, was aware of this and tried to make his time at home as easy and calm as she found possible. Her gratefulness, she hoped, would thus be clear.

One of these weeks, however, was relatively different from the rest, for Adelaide had felt ill. Her mornings were spent over a bowl oftentimes and her evenings were more tiresome than usual. Katarina had felt abandoned when her mother found it difficult to play as she had done as she did not understand; neither did Adelaide. There was one possibility but she dared not assume until there was some level of certainty: she would leave it three more days to see whether he monthly cycle was simply late or not coming at all.

Three days passed in quite the same manner. Nicholas had noticed some changes in his wife but he believed it to be financial stress and Adelaide, not quite ready to reveal her assumption, allowed him to think just that. When she had still not yet bled and was still having similar symptoms to her pregnancy with Katarina, Adelaide received all the confirmation she could ask for.

As Nicholas arrived home that evening, Adelaide met him by the door as usual, helping him remove his coat. After being thanked with a gentle kiss on her forehead, Nicholas was led into the parlour.

“I have some wonderful news,” Adelaide began.

“Do tell me; I am disastrous with guessing,” Nicholas laughed in response; Adelaide was all too content to comply.

“I may be with child,” she said. Her husband’s eyes grew large in delight; a moment of hesitation was followed by his gripping her hands in pure excitement.

“Are you quite certain?” he asked.

“As certain as I can be.” The two embraced, feeling more positive than either had in many months under the struggle of finances. “I believe it would be best to keep this to ourselves until the pregnancy develops further; I would loathe hurting people when there is opportunity to keep everyone’s hearts safe.”

“Of course, yes, of course,” Nicholas said; his joyous feelings existing in every syllable he uttered. “I cannot quite believe this all! I am so happy, Adelaide. I am so proud of how you have been in these recent months. We were met with such problems and, though I have been myself so busy, you have kept house and raised Katarina wonderfully.” He paused, noticing Adelaide’s eyes staring into his, their innocence and beauty ever symbolic of her. Brushing a strand of hair that had fallen loose from her bun behind her ear, he continued: “I really appreciate you.”

“You don’t need to say all this,” Adelaide said, dropping her eyes nervously to the floor.

“I do,” he lifted his chin up with his finger and thumb, forcing her eyes back to his as he softly kissed her. For a moment, it was just the two of them in their minds; their financial problems dissipated into the air and the sounds around them became silent. "I adore you, Adelaide." Unsure of quite how to respond to such an innocent and sweet statement, she merely smiled in response, lowering her eyes as she would have done in her girlhood. "Don't look away." The words barely left his lips, so quiet and well-meaning they were. They stared so intently into the other's eyes that the pupils in and colouring blurred into one hazy image, but it did not matter, for both knew those iris' and lines more so than their own.

It seemed that the joyful promise of a new child in the household was enough to distract from the problems of adulthood and caring financially for a family and home;

smiles were more common and laughter heard more. For the first time in what had felt to be an entirely own lifetime of itself, a sense of hope was writhing in the walls of the home. There was the face of liberty prising through the front door.

However, as it usually goes, when something wonderful happens, something of quite the opposite nature bears its teeth. Only a week following the conversation I have only just presented to you, a terrible incident occurred which I shall not describe in detail so as to save you some of the suffering that our dear protagonist initially faced alone. Instead, I shall leave you to learn of the horrible event as Nicholas himself did.

He had come home, feeling generally positive about the company's gradual growth. The sound of a whistle even graced the hall, making his wife aware of his presence as she greeted him a moment later, taking his coat and kissing his cheek meekly.

"You seem happy," she said, finding comfort in those features she had fallen in love with.

"I am rather happy this evening, I can admit," he said, his smile beaming. "Are you quite alright yourself, dear? You look a little tired."

"Something happened and I'm quite unsure how to tell you, for no matter the place not time it leaves my lips, I know in certainty that its effect will not change," she began, the concern already on his face; he could not help it, for he loved her so dearly that any danger or misfortune that could occur would be troubling indeed to his mind. "This afternoon, early afternoon I should say, I was preparing the dinner when I felt something strange." She paused.

"Yes?" Nicholas asked.

"I lost it. I lost our baby." Her lips quivered, trembling under the heavy layer of emotion and her eyes struggled to stay open. She had only just now been forced to admit the fact out loud and her mind processed it all over again, though this time with the memory of the moment in addition. Nicholas found himself quite speechless and grounded in shock, his eyes locked onto a spot behind his wife, slowly dropping down. "I'm so sorry." Adelaide cried. Wanting to give her words of support but finding himself unable to, he settled instead for holding her tightly; they would be in this moment as one.

Katarina ran down the hallway, not old enough yet to understand the severity of the situation or the remorse on the countenance's of her parents. Her innocent smile was appreciated all the same, however, and their daughter became a beacon of light and hope. The two adults dropped to their knees and embraced Katarina, creating a small huddle of emotions upon the floor.

"Food!" Katarina squealed from within the hold.

"Yes, we should probably dine," her mother said, leading the little bundle of excitement towards the kitchen. Before turning into the room, Adelaide turned round to see her husband but he had not yet moved from the front door; he stood frozen with a solemn look. "Nicholas?" she prompted, her sweet voice echoing slightly down the hall.

"Yes," Nicholas woke from his thoughts. "Yes, I'm coming."

The dinner, though simply divine in taste, was eaten in silence; even Katarina entertained herself silently. There was so much unspoken between Adelaide and Nicholas that it was difficult for complete comfort to be achieved by just a simple glance across the table. If it were not for Katarina, both agreed to themselves that they would have brought it up right there at the dinner table so as to feel even just a hint of support.

Katarina, for this very reason, was put to bed an hour earlier than usual, though she was told that it was very late indeed so as to make the child accept being tucked in with little reluctance. Other than demanding a story to be told before she would even think of closing her eyes, the task was completely relatively quickly, and Nicholas and Adelaide met in their bedroom to discuss further of the sad news. They were both sat upon the bed, nightclothes on, and each held their body in the same way: hunched a little with their arms supporting their body and their feet touching the floorboards.

"How are you feeling?" Nicholas asked.

"Empty," she replied. Nicholas nodded his head slowly in agreement.

"It feels awfully odd, doesn't it?" he began. "Though we are sitting here in this very moment mourning a loss, we have neither gained nor lost anything."

"You sound as though you are Felicity," Adelaide whispered.

"She always does sound rather wise at times, especially for one who'd rather a day writing by a stream dirtying her stockings than with the best society."

"She does, I suppose, though I never thought of it in such a way as you have just described," she said. "I imagine Aunt Augusta would have quite a different response had she known."

"Your Aunt Augusta would most likely be in such a torment of emotions that she may find her deathbed," Nicholas chuckled.

"Now, that is quite impossible!"

"I do believe that she will outlive us all," Nicholas suggested, with a hint of sincerity.

"I hope not! She has such audacity for such a short lady."

"Adelaide Ramsey!" Nicholas gasped at his wife's comment.

"I tell nothing but the truth," she smiled proudly.

"If you say so," he replied. "Look," he continued. "Of course, this is very upsetting news and we are allowed to be disheartened by it. However, we have a lifetime together to expand our family and for Katarina to have siblings; there should be no reason to charge for quick opportunity."

"What about the finances?"

"This would only have helped us in the long term and, with Lady Augusta's strong will, it would be in the very distant long term that we could claim any financial benefit. As for now, the company is improving with every day that goes by so do not worry if you can help it." Adelaide nodded in response, grateful for his words. "We are not far from the end of our troubles."

"And the beginning of something new and wonderful?"

"Exactly." He kissed her forehead, eyes beaming and hands held tightly. "Come, let's get into the sheets. It is might cold and I'd rather keep the use of my toes if possible."

"Oh, Nicholas, you have such a weakness for dramatics," Adelaide teased.

"And you, my dear Addie, have a weakness for being beautiful," he replied, holding his arm for her to lay down next to him.

"I just had a thought," she began. "Our baby is with Phyllis."

"Phyllis will care for them well, we can be sure of that."

"I do miss her immensely," Adelaide tried to think of the last words she had said to her sister but no memory came to mind. "I feel as though I'm forgetting her, Nicholas. I don't want to forget her."

"You won't. You've had a difficult day; I'm sure that you will be able to think of her easily when your mind is more clear. Even I can picture her as she always was. And remember, one day you will be reunited; until then, embrace more of what you have right now. Think of how tomorrow, when it comes, you shall have our little Katarina, in all her excitement, to spend the day with. Then, I will return home in the early evening and you will be surrounded by even more love, for you are abundant in that feeling."

"Are you sure you are not really Felicity?" Adelaide asked. "You sound so much like her today that I quite fear you really have somehow performed such a transformation."

"I hope these comparisons to your sister come from positive connotations?" he laughed.

"You need not worry, Nicholas, for I mean only beautiful things by it."

"If that is truly the case, I can sleep happy," he said, pausing after to blow out the candle on their bedside. "Good night, my love."

~ Chapter Nine ~

Nicholas had been correct in his declaration that the company was on a journey to stability for, only a week following their discussion had the statistics been so wonderfully positive that celebrations were had in the office. Furthermore, for the first time in many months, Nicholas had returned home earlier than usual, arriving in the late afternoon rather than the early evening, and had such a smile upon his countenance that Adelaide could not help but return the joy herself. They embraced lovingly before the door had even been closed, consequently allowing a brush of cold air to reside in the hallway. Neither cared for internal temperatures, however, for, though no words had been spoken, both knew that his early return and content features could only mean one circumstance.

"Oh, is this the end?" Adelaide asked, wide-eyed and youthful.

"It is, my dear," he replied, finally closing the door and beginning to take his coat off.

"Here, let me help," the coat was discarded on the peg along with his scarf. "We were just in the process of preparing dinner. I know it isn't usual but, if you would like, you could join us?" She waited for a moment, unsure of what answer to expect.

"I think I shall," he said. "I've always been curious what you get up to in that kitchen. Besides, maybe I have a talent for cooking that has been unknown all these years."

"If you do, then I shall resent your natural ability for the rest of our lives," Adelaide replied. "For something I've done every day for as long as I can remember, I am so awfully terrible at it. Don't laugh, Nicholas! We can't all be useful to society, or, in this case, the other kitchen staff."

"No, no, of course not!" he laughed in reply. "You need not stress over it though, for you are a wonderful mother and companion." A moment was spent where only a small glance was exchanged between the two. This was followed by an entrance into the kitchen, where Nicholas was met with confused look by the two staff who were preparing the dinner.

"Sir," they curtseyed.

"No need for that societal nonsense! Now, what are we cooking?" he said it with such a jovial voice that the two women had to look to each other, their eyes signalling assistance with producing a response, for both were still in shock from his very presence within the room. "I'm completely serious, I promise you."

"Pork, sir," replied one.

"It is jolly good then that all is well to afford such meat at this time in the year," he said, not quite realising how this could be taken as rude. However, despite his lack of experience in the kitchen, he soon managed to be of some assistance, though his followed a rough beginning where I must admit that he caused more trouble than necessary.

Over the following weeks, the husband and wife spent many moments together, the success of the company allowing Nicholas more time away from the office. This was the most time that the two had spent together since their marriage nearly five years ago and it had felt long overdue by both parties involved.

It was on one fine morning where the sun was not as harsh as it usually was at such a cold time of the year that a picnic had been planned. A wicker basket of small treats had been compiled by Adelaide in the early morning hours and the two had set out on a walk through the gardens to find a suitable seating area. Finding level ground that was not severely damp nor covered by the shade of a tree proved quite difficult and a half hour was dedicated alone to this task. However, the time spent was deemed worthy when the most picturesque area had been acquired; it was surrounded by willow trees, though none that interrupted where the two would sit, and the ground was a soft layer of green, neither too muddy nor steep. A blanket of cloth had been laid across the ground, the basket placed toward the back and between the two bodies who sat facing one another.

"It is so beautiful," Adelaide said.

"Though not as warm as one could hope," Nicholas added, pulling his coat about him more tightly.

"We can't expect much more until the summer months. None the matter, I am grateful to be here all the same."

"As am I, don't mistake me," he said. "Now, I am rather curious to discover what is within this basket of yours. I can smell berries and pastries but my nose may deceive me."

"Nicholas Ramsey," Adelaide teased. "If you would like to open the basket, you may do! We need not wait if you are hungry."

"Wonderful, for I am most starved!" He opened the basket with no hesitation, laying out its inhabitants on the blanket.

"Did you not at all before we left?" she inquired.

"I believed I had better save room for the scrumptious delights you have prepared for the both of us, and I was quite right to do so, for there is such a large quantity before me!"

"I suppose I packed a little more than necessary," Adelaide admitted.

"My darling, when you have spent so many months living as you have done, I think you are perfectly valid in enjoying the moments we can delight in that we could not before." Adelaide thought back to the previous months. They had given up much in the name of stability due to the company's temporary failures that now, as she looked back, she realised just how much. At the time, it had felt nothing less than necessary but now, all she could feel was grateful that the time of desperation had passed.

The picnic had been the beginning of many intimate moments spent between the two of them but certainly had not been the last. I shall not bore you, my dear reader, with describing to you each moment in itself, nor shall I prise into the privacy of such darling humans more than necessary. Yet, I shall tell you of one more before I continue.

Not so many weeks following the picnic, Nicholas had been convinced to agree to a lesson of painting by his wife. Despite not having any talent of a high degree, Adelaide's simplistic attempts were of a beautiful nature and she found much enjoyment in creating them when she had time to herself. Of course, with such a young child to care for, time's such as this were not common.

Two easels had been set up in the parlour room. The preferred setting was out of doors but the weather did not permit this and so, a view from the window was to be an obstruction. Nicholas had been stood before his canvas for such a time, quizzically peering through the glass and at the paint. Adelaide already had some green structures forming and he could not comprehend how she had already done so much.

"Adelaide, perhaps you had better help," he suggested.

"I was wondering how long you would silently suffer for before asking," she replied, placing her paintbrush in a cup of water. "Now, do you see the tree clearly enough?" He nodded. "It may look quite difficult to translate it onto the canvas and so you must simplify it by creating shapes. You see how the branches form an oval of sorts and then the trunk is merely a rectangle." Her fingers traced their lines in the air and, although he listened, Nicholas could look no further than her fingertips. Reaching out his own, he clasped gently onto her fingers, leaning down his head to kiss her hand. "Oh, Nicholas."

"You were saying?" he smiled.

"Yes, of course, I was saying," she began. "You look for the shapes as a beginning and gradually add to what you have until it resembles something similar to what you wish. You shall get nowhere if you do not begin at all."

"I suppose I fear ruining the canvas," he admitted.

"You shall not do anything of the sort," was the response. "Now, do you feel confident enough to begin?"

"Perhaps not but I shall try," he said, picking up the paintbrush. Adelaide did the same, though glanced at Nicholas' canvas, curious to see what he what do. She watched as a green oval was painted and a brown rectangle, and, though she continued with her own piece, she would glance over every few minutes to note the progress he was making. At some moment, unknown to her, he had bypassed her and had completed such a realistic image of a tree that Adelaide had to exclaim:

"Nicholas, that is simply wonderful!" he looked innocently at what he had achieved, quite in disbelief that he, Nicholas Ramsey, had been responsible for such artistry, especially having never even held a paintbrush before. "I am so proud," she said, clasping his hand.

"I must admit that I am quite proud myself, though I do not mean it to be vain."

"That is far from vanity," Adelaide said. "Would it be terribly rude if I were to say I am pleasantly surprised at your talent?"

"Perhaps but I was of the same mind and so I cannot condemn you without condemning myself and that I cannot do," he said. "However, a tree is one thing and the scenery around it is another. I fear I have reached my artistic limit here and it would be futile to continue."

"Are you speaking from a place of fear or boredom?"

"Why, Adelaide, what do you accuse me of?" Nicholas teased. "Though, to answer your question, I suppose a morsel of both."

"Well, I propose that we finish here for today and, when opportunity presents itself, we continue, for I am rather intrigued to see your piece finished."

"I could say the same for yours," he said, squinting his eyes and turning his head to make out her painting.

Adelaide, fully aware of his usual antics, playfully pushed his arm. "I jest. I jest."

"Jest all you like Mr Humorous, but without my excellent teaching ability, you would be in possession of nothing more than a plain canvas, lacking any paint, let alone substance."

"In that you are correct and so I thank you dearly for my lesson," he said. "Now, we should tidy away the paint so that Katarina doesn't create a piece of her own." The paint was tidied and the child acquired. She found herself in a rumble of laughter after learning that her very own father was responsible for the painting but was very soon distracted by a rumble of a different sort: one of hunger. Nicholas, most exhausted by his afternoon of painting, left the cooking to the staff and Adelaide and retired to his office to look over a few sheets from the office. It felt such a relief to complete work tasks without the pressure of failure to both his colleagues and to his family; he had not one horrid bone in his body which could be content with himself had he caused them any permanent pain; the temporary struggle they had been practically forced to endure on his part had already left him with immense guilt. Despite this, it had also filled him with a gratitude and a realisation of the strong woman whom he had as a wife.

As a youth, he had been taught by a father who was cold and harsh in comparison to Mr Thorpe and had learned that marriage was a transaction of finances, status and property. He had learned now, however, that it was instead a transaction of perpetual happiness and trust in a person that he had never known, or even hoped to have known, before. His meeting Adelaide had proven such a wonderful circumstance that he was quite grateful of her positive influence on him. He had often wondered what wasteful life he would have lived had he not had the pleasure of Adelaide's presence as his wife. She was of immense importance to him.

~ Chapter Ten ~

A visit to the Thorpe Hall had been long overdue and so, as the February sun began to set, a carriage brought Nicholas, Adelaide, and even little Katarina to the home. The small child had been only loud and excited and, since the three were confined to the carriage, this became quite tedious after only a few minutes. However, both parents agreed that seeing Katarina in such high spirits was worthy of her behaviour. The smile that she bore had such innocence and delight that it would be cruel to silence her, particularly when the journey was rather long for such a young girl.

"Look at that horse!" she squealed, as their carriage was passed by one of much more grandeur than their own with a horse of a much worthier breed. Nicholas noticed it before it could pass by out of sight and had to agree that it was relatively beautiful for a horse. "Mammy, did you see?"

"I did not have the chance before it galloped past but I'm sure it was wonderful," she replied.

"Maybe we should buy another horse now that all is well," Nicholas pondered, more to himself that to his listeners but Adelaide replied all the same.

"Our horse is perfectly practical."

"Practical, indeed," he began. "But you saw Katarina's reaction to that specimen. Imagine, if that is what a three year old thinks at the sight of it, what a grown adult would think. It would look awfully grand."

"Have you been talking to my Aunt Augusta?" she queried, noting how the old woman would have been all too keen to spend frivolously on a horse if it were to present her estate as well-kept.

"Can we not talk of her on this trip if possible?" he asked as politely as he could manage. "I feel as though I have heard her name so much that she is forever haunting any conversation. She can be so ghastly."

"She means well and we must remember that," Adelaide prompted. "She offered to help us once and, although it wasn't wonderful as short term assistance, it was very considerate of her in a general sense."

"As much as I am reluctant to admit it, I suppose you are right," he began, thinking upon their last year. "I'm sorry. I'm not feeling too patient this morning and being cooped up in here has not helped."

"Do not worry, we shall be home soon."

"Home?"

"You know what I mean, it will always be home in some sense or another, just as our home is also home. I suppose that was a strange way to word it but what I mean to say is that a person can have more than one home. If you were to ask Felicity, she would say that a home is not a place at all, more so a person, and whether that be another or yourself depends entirely on each individual. Isn't is odd how Felicity, though still young, has such a way with words and even life? Even now, I feel as though I barely have a hold."

"That's simply absurd," Nicholas said. "You are exquisite and much more charming than your sister, if I may so."

"You may, though I perhaps would not tell Felicity so," she laughed. "I cannot wait to see them all. Even Felicity has persuaded Mr Giles to stay. I cannot wait to learn more about him. I've not had many moments to speak directly with him and I must admit, I have been curious for quite some time as to his character."

"I cannot say I have put much thought into it but I do look forward to talking with him."

"Will Auntie Phyllis be there?" Katarina asked, her large beady eyes looking up at them both for an answer.

"Auntie Phyllis is in heaven now, dear, do you not remember?" Nicholas said. Adelaide smiled at him in gratitude.

"Oh, I forgot," she said, drooping her eyes in a disappointed manner. "Why does Heaven have to be so far away?"

"That is a question I would very much like to know the answer to myself."

"You know," Adelaide began. Unsure of whether or not she could continue, she gave herself a moment to compose her words before speaking again. "Auntie Felicity used to tell me that Heaven was in the stars."

"*In* the stars?" Katarina wondered.

"Yes. She told me that each person, when they first came to Heaven, was given their own star to live in so that they could watch us from above." Nicholas had never been privy to this before and so he appeared to have very much the same countenance as his daughter.

"I want to live in a star."

"Perhaps you will one day but hopefully not for a very long time," Nicholas said, resuming his position and allowing Adelaide time, as he could not know for sure whether the mention of Phyllis had caused any reaction.

"Ah, there is the house! We are here!" he said and Katarina bounded from the seat to look out the carriage window.

The carriage stopped outside Thorpe Hall. Nicholas left the carriage first and, after lifting Katarina out, held out his hand for Adelaide to take.

"It feels so wonderful to be home," Adelaide said, her voice simple and appreciative as she reminded herself of her memories. The house looked as picturesque as it always had, even as beautiful as it was when the first generation of Thorpe's to make home there resided within its walls. It was no longer just a house; it was a history.

"Adelaide!" called a young girl from the front door. Kitty ran down the garden path, excited and youthful as ever, but her hair was tied back in a strict fashion that her sister had never seen before. This small change, despite its simple nature, caused such fear and concern in Adelaide that she found she could not step further from the carriage. Kitty had ran from the door to the carriage and embraced her sister, who could not return the hug in her confusion. As her younger sister pulled away, Adelaide ran her fingers through a reluctant piece of hair that hung down Kitty's face.

"Kitty, your hair?" she asked in a calm manner.

"Isn't it so grown-up?" her sister replied with such an air and poise that the questioning thoughts only increased.

"Well, yes," she stuttered. "That is rather the point, you are only sixteen? Indeed, I did not style my hair in such a manner until Nicholas and I had married." However, before Kitty could provide her sister with a response, another figure appeared in the doorway - it was Nathaniel Edmunds. Now, dear reader, in the case that you are not familiar with the story of Felicity in as much detail as would prove suitable for such an entrance, I should tell you as much is necessary. Before Felicity had partook in a union with Mr William Giles, she had been certainly good friends with Mr Edmunds, who lacked the social standing to even be considered an appropriate husband. Once Mr Giles and Felicity were married, Nathaniel reacted in such a crude manner that the friendship was lost altogether. And so, I believe you may begin to understand why Adelaide was curious to know why he was here in her family home once more, as though he had not behaved horribly in the last few months to her sister. She had expected to be unfortunate enough to see him about the town but never would she have thought him to be within Thorpe Hall.

"Kitty!" he called, his voice dominant and cold. Kitty turned at the sound.

"We should go inside," she said, an excitement in her words. "There is something you must know!" Adelaide's hand was taken a hold of and she was led into the parlour where an array of people were either sat or stood gathered around the edges of the room. There were all the members of the immediate Thorpe family with the addition of Nicholas, William and Nathaniel. Seeing him was still so odd to her that Adelaide looked to find Felicity in the small crowd in the hopes that her reaction would perhaps begin to explain, for Felicity was not wonderfully talented at hiding her true feelings on a subject and her countenance would reveal all. However, although her face was most certainly representative of her own fear, Adelaide could not translate it.

"Ah, Adelaide, dear!" Mrs Thorpe rose from her position on the chase and wrapped her arms joyfully around her daughter. "You are surprisingly late for one so usually punctual. Even Felicity, and you know how awful Felicity can be, arrived early! Early! Can you believe it?" Adelaide looked to her sister who was playfully rolling her eyes. "And then, when Kitty and Nathaniel arrived I was - " she stopped abruptly, her face turning grave.

"Kitty arrived *with* Nathaniel?" The room was silent with eyes not quite knowing where to look. "What has happened?"

"Maybe you should sit down, dear, and someone will explain, I'm sure!" Mrs Thorpe said, the only one in the room now with a smile, excepting Kitty who had the most large grin one had ever seen. "Now, Kitty, would you like to tell Adelaide, or will you allow your poor mother to finally share the news? You have had the honour of telling everyone else within the room and I am just itching to say it myself."

"Fine, mother," Kitty said, the smile deteriorating only a little, for she was quite used to her mother's ways, as were all the girls.

"Now," Mrs Thorpe turned directly to Adelaide who had been placed next to her mother on the sofa. "You shall never believe that I am to tell you, but tell you I must! Your dear little sister, of only sixteen years, decided it would be such a wonderful idea to elope!" Her voice spoke in an excited voice but her face told the opposite story, for her face had contorted into an intense level of disappointment.

"Eloped?" Adelaide questioned, feeling she had not been given even a morsel of context.

"Eloped!" her mother fell into hysterics.

"With my darling Nathaniel!" Kitty explained, embracing her husband in such an informal manner than her youthful energy contrasted strangely with his rigid hold of himself; he seemed to be looking toward Felicity, at least he had in the moment that Adelaide had looked. Felicity could not even return his eye contact and stared blankly at the ground, biting her lip, lest she say something she would regret. "Isn't it just wonderful?"

"Yes," Adelaide said.

"Congratulations," Nicholas said, offering his hand to Nathaniel.

"Thank you," Nathaniel said.

"If you'll excuse me," Mrs Thorpe cried, leaving the room without waiting for a reaction; her wails in the corridor could be heard by all.

"I do wish mother would be happy about this," Kitty said. "I thought she would love the thought of her only unmarried daughter left finding a husband, especially after Phyllis' death. She should be happy, I know."

"I don't think she quite expected..." Adelaide stopped, deciding she should change her words before she continued. "I don't think she quite expected an elopement. You know how mother loves weddings." She looked at Nathaniel from the corner of her eye; he looked so smug yet there was a sense of resentment in his eyes. Adelaide could not blame him, for all in the household knew that he was perfectly enthralled by Felicity and always would be to some extent.

"Well, she will be all the better if she just thought about how happy it has made me!" Kitty stubbornly replied. "Aren't we so content, Nathaniel?" She looked up at him lovingly, and his reply was so dry that it did not even require words; he simply nodded. "See!" Kitty said. Not a single soul in the room quite knew where to lead from this. As a consequence, the room was filled with an uncomfortable silence and rigidity; the only movement of any kind was of Kitty fawning over her husband. Felicity, despite no longer being of the same mind over Nathaniel as she once was, found herself with a lump in her throat and it took much strength to remain silent. She was not mad with her sister, though she was a little disappointed, but all her hatred of the circumstance was directed completely at Nathaniel. Adelaide could see as much on her face.

"Felicity," Adelaide said, quite unable to remain in the room any longer. "Would you accompany for a walk around the garden?

"I'd love to," replied Felicity, in a reserved manner. The two girls left the room in further silence and only when they had left the building altogether could they breathe again. "I despise it so."

"You do?" her sister asked. "No, of course you do. You are perfectly valid. It was a vile thing of Nathaniel to do."

"You know why he did it, don't you? He couldn't have his way with me so he marries my sister!" Felicity was no longer contained as she had forced herself to be before. Now, she could do nothing to hide her true feelings on the matter. "It was horrid of him. Completely horrid." Felicity sat herself on the wooden bench nestled under a tree, tilting her head into her hands. Adelaide sat by her. "It is not as though I want anything further to do with him. I do not. I am not jealous in any sense."

"We are all aware, do not worry."

"I do worry! Nathaniel can be so horrible and now dear little Kitty will have to endure it until either of them finds their deathbed. She is so young! It is unfair."

"You felt you were too young when you were first promised to William. You wanted nothing more than to be with Nathaniel but you grew to love William, if I am not mistaken."

"I have, that is true, but what has that to do with Kitty and Nathaniel?" Felicity looked to her sister.

"Nathaniel may have done wrong by you but perhaps he will do right by Kitty," even as the words left her lips she did not quite believe it herself. "Kitty is a bright, light-hearted girl and Nathaniel may benefit from that."

"How could you say such things?"

"The elopement has already occurred; there can be no return to what was. We can only hope that some good comes from this."

"I wish I had your optimism, Adelaide," Felicity said. "Why must Nathaniel haunt me so?"

"Nicholas made comment of how he feels Aunt Augusta haunts him on the way here," Adelaide fondly remembered. "I am quite surprised she is not here today."

"Oh, there is the good in today!" and a little colour returned to her cheeks. "As of yet, we have not been graced with the appearance of Aunt Augusta! How divine!"

"She is not as terrible as you all paint her," was the elegant reply. "She has out-dated ideas, yes, but her heart is in the right place. Even you, Felicity, cannot fault her on that."

"I suppose not but all the same I am grateful for her absence!"

"While we speak of marriage, I wanted to ask how William and yourself are?" Felicity seemed so content following the mention of his name. "You look happy."

"I am so happy, dear Adelaide," she said, looking into the distance as she thought. "He is everything I could hope for."

"Then I am mightily glad. Shall we return? It has been so long since I have seen everyone together and there is much to discuss, though let us make a pact that we shall limit conversation of their elopement as much as we find possible."

"I accept!" they laughed heartily as they returned to the parlour where the silence had been replaced by a multiplicity of conversations; even dear old Mrs Thorpe had wiped her tears and was standing by her newly acquired son-in-law.

"Oh, there you are!" Mrs Thorpe had been attracted to the quiet footsteps of her daughters, eager for new people to engage in conversation with. "I was just discussing how far Nathaniel's chosen home is! Tell them, dear. Go on! 34 miles, I dare say! I know options are somewhat limited but surely 34 miles is far too much to carry a daughter away from her dear mother! I've told them they must continue to search until they come to a final decision, just to be certain."

"I'm sure it will make a beautiful home," Adelaide said to Mr Edmunds and Kitty, who stood clinging tightly to his arm as though he would leave if she were to loosen her grip even the slightest. Nathaniel nodded in response.

Adelaide had agreed they would stay for a week so as to spend quality time as it was believed that, now Kitty was married, this would be the last time for a while that they could all be together. It is true that Kitty being so far away was not considered ideal for any member of the Thorpe family, excepting herself, who, having never been much further than the homes of her sisters would not know the true length of 34 miles until it was far too late. However, that would not be for a few more weeks and so the time spent at Thorpe Hall was of Kitty's only concern.

The week entailed a series of walks, both within the grounds of the property and the town itself. These were considered immensely pleasurable for all involved; even Nathaniel was seen with a smile when he and Kitty had entered a fabric shop. He was seen through the window by

Adelaide and Felicity. Each had to admit that he did indeed appear to be in love.

"He probably has far too much pride to show his true affection under the gaze of others," Felicity had said, reluctant still to be fully accepting of the elopement. "His ego was thoroughly bruised and he still hasn't recovered."

On the penultimate day before they were scheduled to return to home, it was Katarina's fourth birthday. It had been agreed by all involved that it would be celebrated at Thorpe Hall with games and fun throughout the day. Katarina, young though she was, had been counting down the days for almost a fortnight and had been terribly defiant the night before. How could one be expected to sleep when such a huge milestone was occurring only the following day?

Each person, in a great effort to make a wonderful day for the child, had obtained a small gift so, when placed all together, a tremendously sized pile had been created on the floor of the parlour. Katarina had exulted such excitement and disbelief that they indeed were all for her that she begun to cry.

"Isn't she such a delight?" Mrs Thorpe said, rejoicing with her hands clasped together. "I baked those cookies myself!" she said to one in particular. The cookies were certainly delicious and enjoyed by all, so much so that a second batch was wished for most ferociously. However, since the day was inclusive of such enjoyment from a variety of activities, they were left forgotten, forever to remain only in the morning of that day.

The following day, still basking the afterglow of such a wonderful day, members of the family began to depart from their beloved family home. Kitty and Nathaniel had been the first to leave, followed closely by Felicity and William. Adelaide had wished to stay a little longer so that she could spend a moment in Phyllis' room to herself. She had sat on her bed and breathed softly as she glanced around the room at what would have been the last thing her dear sister had known. Despite such a mournful thought, Adelaide found more comfort than despair within it and felt close to her sister for the first time following her death. It was only after this that she felt ready to return to her new home.

~ Chapter Eleven ~

Adelaide had found herself in high spirits the weeks following their visit to Thorpe Hall. A return to what reminded her of a childhood of happiness and love had connected her to Phyllis once again and had filled her with a new desire to begin trying for a child once again. Of course, a little fear was mangled with this but she adored seeing Katarina's smile throughout their days spent together and she wished to feel that with more children of her own. It was on Thursday afternoon that she felt ready to tell Nicholas of her recent thoughts.

"I have been thinking upon only one subject as of recently," she began.

"Is that so?" was the response. He too had been having thoughts of trying once again but he could not bear to influence his wife to any degree and had decided that he had better wait for her to bring it up; only then would he declare his support. Since he had known his wife so closely for a great many years now, his suspicions has formed solely by the twinkle in her eye and her breaking the silence in such a way acted as an appearance of confirmation.

"How would you feel about trying again, to be with child?" she asked, her palms a little sweaty from the nervous undertones.

"I would love nothing more," he replied, rising from his seat as she did to hold her tightly. "I would love that." He kissed her forehead, shaking with excitement and love; how did he have such an abundance of love for only one human? It had astounded him before but now, as he held her in his arms so softly, he could think of nothing more than how much this one woman meant to him: she, who had so much kindness to give to the world. She, who could not harm even the smallest creature. She, who was given such grief and handled it with grace and beauty. She, who defined love.

It is my absolute pleasure, my dearest reader, to inform you that Adelaide did indeed find herself with child and Nicholas and herself had been over joyous at the fact. In order to share the news, after they had been quite certain that she would carry through to the end with little risk involved, a dinner was planned for the entirety of their family. Even Aunt Augusta had been invited, but, after learning of how many guests were to be in attendance, she insisted that they dined in her own, for it was much larger and suitable for such a sizeable party of people. She had been gratefully accepted and a date for the 9th day of April had been planned.

"It was such a wonderful idea for us all to dine together," Mrs Thorpe began, as she quite violently cut at her meat, scraping the knife back and forth too many times as she became distracted by her own talking. "I do love seeing everyone together, although it is a shame that our little Phyllis cannot enjoy what we have so graciously been given. Thank you, again, Lady Augusta. You are such a generous lady." The Aunt slowly nodded her head in response while secretly appalled at the woman's table manners; how long did she plan to cut at that one piece of meat for? "And thank you, Nicholas and Adelaide, for planning such an event!"

"You are very welcome, mother," Adelaide replied. Although she was rather nervous to continue, she and Nicholas had confirmed through their eyes that now was a suitable time to share their news. "We must admit, Nicholas and I, that is, that we planned this dinner for a particular purpose. We have something we would love to share with you all." At this, Mrs Thorpe nearly fell from her chair, dropping her cutlery onto the plate and frantically thinking of everything she wanted to hear. Adelaide looked to Nicholas and they both exchanged smiles. Mrs Thorpe grew all the more excited and anxious to hear what they had to say.

"If you've something to say, do not have us waiting over our plates," Lady Augusta said, coldly.

"Of course," Adelaide continued. "I am with child."

"Oh!" Mrs Thorpe found it difficult to remain seated. The smile upon her countenance was so large that her skin was prone to tear if she stretched it anymore.

"I wouldn't say that is entirely suitable conversation for the dinner table," Lady Augusta said. "But I congratulate you all the same."

"Yes, yes," Mrs Thorpe said, straightening herself out. "Not suitable. No. But isn't it just wonderful? Oh, I am so happy!"

Felicity, who had been sat next to her sister, decided on a different approach than her mother and great Aunt. She placed her hand on top of Adelaide's that rested upon the table, and said quietly:

"That is magnificent news, I cannot wait to meet them."

"Thank you, Felicity, thank you," she replied, feeling grateful and emotional all at once. She knew that while her family consisted of such unique persons, each one was content in their own way with the news and showed it in a different way. While Mrs Thorpe exulted far too much energy, her Aunt Augusta showed little but restraint, and while Felicity was simple but meaningful, Kitty was too happy to speak. This was her family, the people she loved. She felt no fear at having her child becoming part of them.

~ Chapter Twelve ~

The year had brought with it new marriages and new children; it had been, as a consequence, one of marvellous events. Kitty and Nathaniel's wedding had soon be accepted after they had attended numerous family occasions and been seen to be relatively smitten with each other. Felicity soon learned to forgive his behaviour and focuses instead on the maturity he had nurtured, even if she had been a little regretful that it had not been for her. However, she felt more than content with William and believed that all had occurred as had been intended.

The house some 34 miles from Thorpe Hall had been purchased by Mr Edmunds, for the building and grounds was simply divine. Even Mrs Thorpe, following only one visit, had declared that she had been expeditious in her judgement, focusing only on the distance rather than its ability to provide a happy home from her daughter and son-in-law. It was of a moderate size with tall windows and ivy running along the brickwork, with a beautiful garden blooming with flowers. In a way, it reminded Kitty of her former home and for this, she was eternally happy. Although she had not found this happiness in the usual way, she had found it, and that was all that mattered.

Within this year, Elizabeth Mae Giles had been born and she was so daintily beautiful that Adelaide and Nicholas had found themselves further in anticipation for their own child. They had watched in awe as Katarina interacted with the small babe and felt such a warm feeling in their hearts knowing that they would see this every day when Katarina had a sibling.

That very day, when their own child was born, came some months after this. As Adelaide held her child close to her chest, Nicholas looked down on the both, with little Katarina stood by him.

"It's a boy," Adelaide said, crying sweetly from the love that she felt. Seeing her husband and both her children was such a heartfelt experience for one who considered herself family orientated and she accepted all the embraces offered by her little family with such love. She felt as though the happiness she experienced in this moment would never be equalled and, in that, I am afraid there is some truth.

The child was christened Henry Ramsey soon after his birth and this had the effect of causing a visit from Lady Augusta. She had arrived unexpected and somewhat unwanted, for she was difficult to host, and had demanded a tea within only a minute of being seated. The drink had been brought to her in quick pace and laid out before her.

"I will not begin with some idle talk of unimportant matters," she said to Mr and Mrs Ramsey. "I have come to discuss the matter of my will." Nicholas and Adelaide exchanged a small glimmer of a look with one another as she spoke. "I spoke before of a particular circumstance that would permit me to increase what I have decided for you to inherit. This circumstance, as you know, was to birth a boy, or, more specifically, an heir. As you have done so, I would like to confirm that I am still happy to do so, for I would never be so cruel as to go back upon a promise I had made."

"Thank you, Aunt Augusta," Adelaide said graciously. "We are so grateful but we do hope that you will not depart us in the near future and remain in excellent health." The latter part had been somewhat of a lie but only to a small degree, for Adelaide cared too much for people to fully wish a death upon them.

Kitty and Nathaniel had been promised much the same thing by the Lady Augusta and I can assure you that Mr Edmunds had not the same and polite reaction as Adelaide had provided. He cared little for the woman who had denied his union with Felicity for so many years, even if he now found himself a married man.

And so our story ends, for now.

Printed in Great Britain
by Amazon

41179006R00111